ABOUT THE AUTHOR

James Warden was a teacher for forty years and retired in 2006. He now enjoys his retirement as much as he enjoyed his time in the education service and is catching up on those things which he left undone and ought to have done – in particular, his writing. He writes every morning between nine o'clock and noon, for thirty-six weeks of the year.

He is fortunate enough to be able to act in several Norwich theatres – the Maddermarket, the Sewell Barn and, with the Great Hall Players, at the Assembly House – and this experience informs his writing. His stage adaptation of Laurie Lee's *As I Walked Out One Midsummer Morning* was performed at the Sewell Barn Theatre in November 2009. His original play, *Letters from a Boy in the Trenches*, which was based on the letters of a WW1 soldier, was performed in Marchington, Staffordshire in 2015.

James is married – for the second time – and lives in Norfolk. He and his wife travel as much as possible. They have visited Italy (where they were married in 2002) several times, Canada, Bermuda, Egypt, India, the Czech Republic, New England, Poland, Slovenia, Antarctica, the Falkland Islands, Alaska, the Galapagos Islands, Australia and Switzerland. In 2018, they travelled across the USA on Route 66. They have also taken several holidays in various Mediterranean resorts

– the basis for his first novel, *Three Women of a Certain Age*, which was published in July 2010, and *Bingham Goes to Cannes*, to be published in 2024.

During his years in education, he wrote about twenty play scripts for children. These included the one that formed the basis for his children's story, *The Great Gobbler and his Home Baking Factory at the North Pole*, which he wrote in 1982 and published in December 2010.

He has three sons by his first marriage, and they inspired two of his novels – *The Vampire's Homecoming*, which was published in 2011, and *The One-eyed Dwarf*, published in 2012. With them and his first wife, he also travelled to the southern states of North America, France, Germany (West and East), Estonia and what was Czechoslovakia.

WRITING BY JAMES WARDEN

Stories of Our Time
Three Women of a Certain Age (2010)
The Age of Wisdom (2015)
Swinging in the Sixties (2016)

'Tales of Mystery and Imagination'
The Vampire's Homecoming (2011)
The First Rendlesham Incident (2017)
The Search for Edwin Drood (2020)

Stories for Children
The Great Gobbler and his Home-Baking Factory at
the North Pole (2010)
The One-eyed Dwarf (2012)

Biography
The Boy in the Photograph:
Bill Pieri's autobiography (2014)
A Child of the Fifties:
autobiography of my childhood (2017)

Plays
As I Walked Out One Midsummer Morning
*(Adapted with the permission of Laurie Lee's
estate and performed at the Sewell Barn
Theatre in Norwich in November 2009.)*

Letters from a Boy in the Trenches
*(Adapted from the letters home of Sydney Harrison
and performed by the
Marchington Amateur Dramatic Society
in November 2015.)*

BINGHAM PURSUES A MINISTER'S CLERK

BY

JAMES WARDEN

Grosvenor House
Publishing Limited

This book is published by
Grosvenor House Publishing Ltd
Link House
140 The Broadway, Tolworth, Surrey, KT6 7HT.
www.grosvenorhousepublishing.co.uk

This book is a work of fiction. Any resemblance to
people or events, past or present, is purely coincidental.

A CIP record for this book
is available from the British Library

ISBN: 978-1-83975-536-1

Chapter One
THE GRAMMAR SCHOOL BOY

George Bingham always enjoyed the Autumn Fair, which followed hard on the heels of the Harvest Supper and took place on the field adjacent to the little church of St Mary Magdalene in the village of Northfield, near Ipswich in Suffolk.

His pleasure was embedded in many memories: memories of the village and of the church. He and Lina had been married in the church over thirty years before, and it was where each of their four children had attended Sunday school during the spring years of their lives. Northfield was the village where his children had grown to adulthood, where they ran and played, where their first friendships had been forged, their first music teacher found, where they'd joined the Scout and Guide movements, watched (and then played) cricket on the local field, helped with the harvest and climbed their first haystack, shared an under-age drink with their friends in the bar at the back of The Barley Mow.

The honey had flowed that summer – the summer of 2016 – and his bees had produced enough to see themselves through the coming winter as well as providing him with enough to sell three hundred jars at the fair and to set some aside some for his family and friends.

He looked around at the other stalls as he divided the fifteen hundred pounds equally between his inner pocket, his side pocket and the bag the church treasurer had provided. They were all in full swing: the tombola, the apple-bobbing, the cakes, the conserves, the wood carvings, the crazy golf, the bouncy castle, the barbecue and the mass of produce from the Harvest Festival itself. Northfield's Autumn Fair was well known, and people had poured in from the surrounding villages and from the town, parking their cars where they could once the small carpark at the village hall was full.

Bingham felt tired, and his shoulder was still playing up after the incident with the drug dealer. He'd slide quietly into the little church and wait for the bustle to die down: through the kissing gate in the hedge, across the churchyard, winding his way between the graves. The door of St Mary Magdalene was always unlocked; it was the kind of Suffolk village where residents were able to leave their back doors on the latch, and many did, out of habit or familiarity.

On his way he passed the grave of Lina's parents: Percy Bird (1915 – 1993) and Eva Bird nee Marinacci, (1916 – 2002). He remembered Lina insisting on the children being baptised in the Roman Catholic Church of the same name in Ipswich out of respect for her mother, a devout Catholic who Lina had accompanied to Mass every week until the day she died.

But Lina saw the church as part of the community and her community was Northfield and its people. She had led the way in their social lives, as women tend to do, following her mother's footsteps into village life. Unlike Bingham, she knew most of the villagers, partly because of her involvement and partly because

Northfield had been the home of her childhood, her father owning and working the land known as Bob's Farm that was now their home.

Bingham had been content to sit and watch, waiting on the verges until needed; but, inevitably, he too had been drawn into the life of the village, a community where summer fetes, autumn fairs and seasonal celebrations played an integral part.

Although an atheist of the reluctant sort, Bingham enjoyed the services he attended, appreciating the theatricality of the church's ritual and the sense of peace he acquired whenever he sat and contemplated the state of his soul – in his case, probably not an immortal one. Simply sitting in one of the pews, listening to the calm of ages, brought him a sense of contentment and wonder.

He looked up at the stained-glass window in the west wall, the one of Mary Magdalene herself, and wondered. How many people had found refuge here from a world that often seemed hostile to them or, at the best, uncaring? There were burdens one must shoulder for oneself but there were many that seemed unbearable, if only for a time, and the church – the church of the village, at least – offered sanctuary and benediction.

He cast his eyes upwards and the series of figures on the hammer beam ends in the roof looked down upon him: the angels in the nave, the kings and queens in the chancel. Their closeness took his breath away. If only.

Even with his lack of hearing, Bingham heard the door open – the latch was too heavy to lift silently – and knew who it was without turning around. He'd almost expected the interruption.

"I thought you might be here."

Lina sat beside him in the pew. If she knew where he was, Bingham wondered why his wife found it necessary to find him. There must still be plenty to do at the fair and she was an integral part of the organisation: the putting up and the taking down. He smiled, squeezed her hand, but said nothing.

"Mabel isn't here, Bing."

So, there was a reason; Bingham had thought that her coming was simply one of the vagaries of womanhood, the need to know.

"I realise you said you'd never interfere with an on-going investigation, Bing, but I wondered if …"

Lina paused deliberately, knowing he wouldn't refuse her request. He said nothing; his mind was still on Mary and the angels watching him. He'd had an easy life. He'd been very, very lucky; but occasionally he'd needed a guardian angel, and one of them was sitting beside him now.

"Robert's still missing."

He knew Mabel Courtney only vaguely, her son even less so. She was a plump, busy, little woman who always ran the Mothers Union stall, the one that offered items the women had knitted, woven or embroidered over the previous year, anything from a comb case to a patchwork quilt. She was as an essential part of the church and the autumn fair as were Mary Magdalene and his jars of honey.

"I must get back now. Do you know where Mabel lives?"

"Remind me."

"It's one of the old cottages along Lower Road: the one with the stable door."

Bingham kissed his wife goodbye, and she hurried back to the fair. He wondered how many of the old cottages had a stable door. Lina's faith in him was always uplifting.

Lower Road went out of the village to the west, leading by several farms and eventually to the outskirts of Ipswich. It also took him close to the allotments, five of which were cultivated by his friend, Phil Bassett, the man who had taught him all he knew about beekeeping and whose help that summer had been indispensable.

Robert Courtney had been missing for several months along with a quarter of a million pounds from some Treasury budget. There had been the usual splash in the papers, the usual rush and tear of reporters in the village and then all had gone quiet. The police seemed unable to find the young man, which had puzzled Bingham and annoyed his friend, Simon Brockie, the retired Detective Chief Inspector, who seemed disinclined to discuss the matter.

None of the villagers had taken against the young man's mother, which had reaffirmed Bingham's faith in human nature. Several – including Lina and the local vicar, Clemency Freeman – had rallied round to support Mabel Courtney in her hour of need. Lina, who disliked women's groups intensely, had readily turned up at several Mothers Union meetings in support of the lady.

This muddle of thoughts poured through Bingham's head as he sought the old cottage with the stable door. The row of dwellings was set back from the road and at a lower level, and Bingham remembered that all had been prone to flooding in severe storms until the council had been forced to improve the drainage system following years of protests and petitions.

He tried to clear his head; he was becoming localised and it disturbed him. Better to simply stand back and admire the long front gardens replete with campanula, baby's breath, meadow rue, Vatican sage, geraniums, hollyhocks and purple-leaved violets.

He found what he thought was Mabel Courtney's cottage. It was the only one with the top half of the stable door open, the only one showing any signs of habitation: everyone else was at the fair or, in the case of several of the men, avoiding it by working on their allotments.

"A bad afternoon, Mr Bingham: I just couldn't face it. It wasn't the villagers but the townspeople I didn't want to see me."

"You think they would remember?"

"It's what I can't forget – my son branded as a thief and on the run from the police."

"Did Lina say I was coming to see you, Mabel? You seem to be expecting me."

"She rang me earlier when I didn't turn up at the fair. Please come in, and I'll make you a cup of tea."

Bingham sat in the small kitchen whose lattice window overlooked – if that could be said of so small a window – the cottage garden. He watched Mabel Courtney brew the tea from loose leaves and remove the lid from the cake tin before serving him at the little table, which was covered with a gingham cloth.

"I don't make cakes as often as I did – not now Robert isn't home at weekends."

"He used to come home every weekend?"

"He would always come once a month – sometimes more often."

"He lived in London during the week?"

"He found himself a flat somewhere in Holborn. He was lucky. Inexpensive accommodation is hard to come by these days in London. I've been down to see it. It's quite nice."

"Did he have any friends there?"

"Yes …"

Bingham noticed the hesitation.

"But?"

"Robert was quite a shy boy. University helped, but he was always more interested in his work than in his social life."

"He went to Oxford, didn't he?"

"Straight from the local grammar school, as it used to be called. They were so proud of him. It was just before they brought in those dreadful tuition fees, otherwise I couldn't have afforded to send him."

"I believe he was at school the same time as my youngest son, Ben."

"He spoke about Ben. They were in the Scouts together."

Bingham suddenly had the mental picture he was striving to gather. Robert Courtney had been naturally shy, rather than reclusive. Bingham remembered seeing him at one of the camps organising the cooking: quite a tall lad, on the lean side with a wedge of curly, black hair. He'd been watchful, a listener as opposed to a talker.

"Maths was his subject?"

"He gained a first-class honours degree in mathematics. They took him on at the Treasury without hesitation. He was training to be an actuary."

Bingham realised how hard the boy must have been working. Training as an actuary took seven years after the student had gained their degree; and then it was a matter of waiting for an existing actuary to retire or drop dead. It was the classic closed shop.

He looked at Mabel Courtney across the table, wondering where Robert had acquired his height. Bingham couldn't recall a father.

"Robert's father was also tall," said Mabel Courtney with a smile, as though she'd put people in the picture many times before. "He died when Robert was three: the same year as Lina's father and with the same disease. It was the year you all came to live at Bob's Farm."

"It must have been a struggle for you."

"We managed. Robert's father had a small pension due to him – death in service, you know – and I got a job with Barclays bank in Ipswich."

"He is your only child?"

"Yes. We started late, rather like you and Lina."

"Where did Robert's father work?" asked Bingham, unsure why the question seemed relevant.

"On the railways. It was different in those days. They looked after their staff and the men's families."

They were getting nowhere, and yet everywhere. Although they hadn't discussed what led to Robert's flight with so much money, Bingham felt he'd known the young man – a distant figure from the past – all his life. He knew how he'd walk, talk and dress; he knew how his little flat in Holborn would be furnished, how his desk at work would look and the places he'd choose to frequent in his off-duty hours. He would have 'off-duty hours' rather than a social life.

He saw Robert and his mother together: Mabel fussing round the young man, in a hurry to wash the clothes she would have insisted her son brought home when he came on that Friday night once a month, her pressing a tin of cakes on him when he went back. He saw Robert slipping the tin gently into a small holdall.

Or did he? Was he jumping to conclusions? Do any of us ever really know another person closely enough to predict their inner life? Knowing Robert Courtney's inner life was what Bingham was after.

"Have the police spoken to you?"

"They've done more than that, Mr Bingham. They ransacked my home – nicely, but ransacked, nevertheless. They even went through my personal drawers."

"What did they take?"

"They went through the whole cottage – not just Robert's room. Robert's flat in London is only a small one and there isn't space for everything, and so he left a lot of his things at home. They took an old diary and his notebooks – all his school notes, Mr Bingham – and some bills and some of his books. I can't see why: they were all about mathematics. Oh, and they took some of his photographs. It didn't make sense. Why would they take a photograph of his father? Old family photographs, Mr Bingham. I hope we get them back one day. They looked everywhere – even under the mattresses, mine as well as Robert's. Oh yes, and they took some of his magazines and journals. They were all about economics and finance. And his trombone! Why would they take his trombone, Mr Bingham?"

Bingham didn't know. The ransacking seemed both random and pointless. He reached across the table and squeezed Mabel Courtney's hand. Her voice had risen, and she was trembling.

"We'll have to find out, Mabel – but only if you call me George."

She laughed and poured him another cup of tea.

"Were these local police officers?"

"I don't know that they were real policemen. They seemed too authoritarian to be local people. They were very imposing. They dropped the search warrant on the table and went about their business without a by your leave."

"They were not in uniform?"

"No, but very smartly dressed."

"How did they arrive?"

"They came in a taxi – two taxis."

"Station taxis?"

"Yes."

"I see. Do you still have the search warrant?"

Mabel Courtney retrieved it carefully from a small cash box that she kept on one of her kitchen shelves beside a potted plant. It had been signed by someone at the Home Office but meant nothing to Bingham. He'd never seen a search warrant in his life. He must ask Brockie.

"Mabel, do you have any idea where Robert is hiding? Be honest with me. Has he been in touch?"

The old lady only hesitated for a moment, and then drew a letter from her apron pocket. The letter, which was typed, simply assured Robert's mother that he was safe and innocent of the theft, that he had no idea why he had been accused or how the money had got into an account in his name. He went on to say that she mustn't worry and that he would fight to clear his name.

"Find him, George, and tell him to give himself up. It's the only way. He can't stay on the run for the rest of his life. He can only clear his name by coming into the open."

"Did Robert have any friends locally?"

"They all moved away when they left university, George. You lose touch when you leave school, don't you, unless you end up living in the same place?"

"I suppose you do."

Bingham, having wandered through Europe for several years after leaving university, had found it to be precisely as Mabel described; when he returned to England, he found no one he'd known as a child or, if he did, they were married and otherwise occupied.

"Did he speak of any of his friends in London – his friends or his workmates?"

"No, not really. Except John – he shared Robert's flat in London. He was an old school friend."

"Did he keep in touch with anyone he knew at university?"

"There was one young man called Alan Vernon. He came here once or twice. I must say, though I shouldn't, that I didn't like him a great deal."

"Why?"

"I'm not sure. He seemed aloof, as though we weren't quite up to his mark. I don't know what Robert saw in him."

"Did Robert have many friends at Oxford?"

"I think so. I think he was happy there. He always came home laughing in the holidays."

"Did he have a girlfriend?"

"No. I told him he ought to get married but he didn't seem interested."

The modern world would make much of that fact, although quite unnecessarily, thought Bingham. His

European wanderings had brought him into touch with many women, none of whom he would have described as a 'girlfriend'. Mothers were always in too much of a hurry to marry you off and your peers – at least, nowadays – in too much of a hurry to determine your sexuality. His generation had avoided the concerns of the peers if not of the mother, although Bingham had managed both.

His weariness overcame him again. He'd stood for several hours selling his honey and found only a few minutes respite in the church before coming to listen to Mabel Courtney's worries. He wasn't unsympathetic – just tired. And there were getting nowhere – a conclusion he'd come to about twenty minutes previously.

"Do you mind if I take a look in Robert's room, Mabel?"

Mabel Courtney was taken aback, perhaps suspecting another search, but led Bingham through to the back parlour from which a flight of narrow stairs led to the two petite bedrooms.

Robert's was exactly as Bingham had imagined it: tidy almost to the point of being old-maidish.

"Is this how the search team left it?"

"It's how Robert liked it. I tidied up after they'd gone. I put everything back in its place."

Among the reading, Bingham noticed *The Economic Journal*, *Mathematical Social Sciences*, the *Quarterly Journal of Economics*, the *Journal of Political Economy* and the *International Journal of Central Banking*. These all had their special place in open box files. The single bed was placed hard against one wall to make for more space in the room. There was a bedside table and lamp and a desk under the one window, which looked out over the front garden and towards the allotments.

"Robert had an old computer, George, but the police took that away. The desk looks empty without it. They took his data sticks as well – I think that's what Robert called them."

A small chest of drawers was the only furniture in the room. Robert Courtney's clothes were hung either on the back of the bedroom door or in a small closet that was curtained off from the room.

To the side of the desk was a bookshelf containing a few novels – all science fiction of the classic or old-fashioned sort: Verne, Wells, Wyndham, Christopher, Kneale and Asimov. There was also a copy of Amis's *New Maps of Hell* but nothing else of a critical nature. The only other book was Phillip Stokes's *Philosophy:100 Essential Thinkers*. Well, the young man had to find his relaxation somewhere. It roused Bingham's admiration that Robert Courtney had gained a place at Oxford working from this very room.

Bingham didn't like to sit down while Mabel Courtney stood and so he gestured her to the desk chair before easing himself down onto the bed, raising both a frown and an eyebrow on the face of the young man's mother.

"Let's suppose – just for the moment and just for the sake of argument – that Robert did move funds from one account to another. Can you suggest why he might have had a reason to do that? Did he ever discuss politics with you? What were his views on government, for example?"

"I don't know what you're getting at, Mr Bingham ..."

"George! Don't be angry with me, Mabel. We have to consider every possibility, and, at this moment, only one presents itself."

"That my boy is a thief!"

"Was there any reason why he might move such a huge sum of money? Was he asked to do so? What authority did he have? Did he operate under a strict system? Did he tend to be cavalier?"

"He always told me he was the Minister's Clerk, but I think he was joking. I can't answer any of those questions, George."

"Neither can I now. What was his boss's name?"

"It was a Sir Herbert Elliot. I do know that."

"And did this man get in touch with you?"

"No. I only found out what had happened from the newspapers."

Mabel Courtney was clearly struggling with the difficulties Bingham had thrown at her. She stood, abruptly, and moved to the window. Her hands twisted the front of her apron as though she was trying to tie knots in the fabric.

"If he were asked to move the money, surely he wouldn't be accused of stealing it? Once the story appeared in the papers, his employers could have refuted it, couldn't they?"

"Yes, they could, if it suited them to do so."

"Why wouldn't it?"

"I don't know. I don't even know that that's what happened; but if Robert didn't place the money in an account bearing his name, someone else did. The question is why and who."

Bingham was feeling shut in. He looked at Robert Courtney's desk and saw the boy, later the young man, sitting there poring over his textbooks. *An Introduction to Calculus*: he remembered his own difficulties with that one at 'O' Level and the teacher explaining to him that the title of any book was best ignored as an indication of the book's content.

He hadn't taught Robert (a fact he regretted at that moment) having chosen to work in what was termed a 'comprehensive' school in those days, where he thought he might be able to help those children less likely to be influenced by their circumstances.

The room closed in on him as it must have closed in so many times on Robert, alone with his books, his mother no doubt fussing around, wondering whether he wanted a drink or whether he'd had enough to eat.

"Can we go into the garden, Mabel?" he asked, suddenly.

The second they passed out through the back-door Bingham felt better. It was a warm day, but a slight breeze took the mugginess out of the air. There wasn't much back garden, but the low, paling fence allowed them to look out over acres of farmland, now under the plough ready for the planting of winter wheat; he heard the cries of seagulls, up from the docks and looking for worms.

"You would like me to find Robert before the police do and persuade him to give himself up so that his innocence can be proved openly?"

"I'm so grateful, Mr Bingham."

"George! I only hope I can oblige, Mabel, but ... you mustn't give yourself any false hopes. Do you understand?"

His pause had prevented Bingham saying what he was thinking: if the constabulary with every technique and resource at its disposal hadn't found Robert Courtney, he didn't see why he should be successful.

"Yes, yes of course, but I'm sure you will find my son."

Bingham wasn't a touchy-feely person, although Lina's influence had amended that deficiency to some degree, but he put his arms round Mabel Courtney and gave her a hug. He wasn't sure why, except that somewhere at the rear of his thoughts was the feeling that this was an unpleasant business, which couldn't end happily.

He bid her goodbye, having obtained a photograph of Robert and the spare key for his London flat she kept in her cash tin, and made his way across Lower Road and so onto the allotment path. He wanted to see Phil Bassett, who would probably be giving his bees one of their autumn feeds. It was late afternoon; the foragers would have returned to the hive; it was the right time to offer them their syrup solution.

Phil had completed his task and was enjoying a pint and a pipe in the little shed he referred to as the 'Officers' Mess'. This shed was the hub of the allotments: its pot-bellied stove provided a companionable place to sit and chat in winter, its security system informed intruders they were under surveillance and provided reassurance to the allotment holders, its fridge was always stocked with Adnams beers and its workbench ensured the winter months were usefully engaged in repairing and constructing hives.

Phil bought all his clothes from charity shops. As each collection wore out, he would simply descend on a shop and select at random whatever he needed, regardless of whether the clothes matched or were even seasonable. Today, Bingham found him dressed in a

French beret, a pair of camouflage trousers, an American check shirt and a red silk scarf that must have cost a fortune new.

Phil stirred his large frame from the cane chair as his friend entered, but Bingham waved him down. Phil's legs had been playing up due to some ill-prescribed statins, and Bingham could see the pain on the younger man's face.

"Help yourself to a beer, George. You've been courting the Widow Courtney, I see."

"Your taste in music is better than your taste in jokes, Phil," replied Bingham.

From a CD player, which stood on a corner shelf of the shed, came the sounds of Britten's *Variations on a Theme of Frank Bridge*. They both enjoyed English classical music and took the occasional trip together to the Aldeburgh Festival.

"How's the shoulder?"

"The doctor said three months and he was near enough, but my bones are old, Phil, and they don't heal quickly. The clavicle still plays me up, especially at night. Without you doing all the graft, I'd never have taken my honey off the hives this year."

"It was nothing."

"It was everything. I couldn't have lifted a super, let alone do the extracting. I'm very grateful. Here's your share."

"I can't accept this, old friend," said Phil unrolling the notes Bingham handed him and counting the five hundred pounds.

"It's a third of what I sold today. The labourer is worthy of his hire. Without you and my grandson, I'd have been stumped."

Phil frowned and then smiled, tucking the notes into his trouser pocket; he wasn't one to argue over a business deal.

"What did you want with the widow? Was it about her son?"

"She wants me to find him before the police do."

"Strange lad – nice boy but strange, if you know what I mean."

"You know him? Go on."

"When he was younger, just after he'd started the grammar school, he and a friend came over and asked if they could do some experiments with snails on the allotments. I'm buggered if I can see why anyone would want to work out the speed of a snail, but they did. They were very exact. They took great care. Everything was recorded in their notebooks: snails on soil, snails on wood, snails on plastic, snails on corrugated iron, snails going up and snails going down – you name it and they measured it. They'd make damn good beekeepers when they grow up if they keep records that precise."

"What was the other lad's name?"

"John Hunt. I remember because it was the same name as the one who climbed Everest in 1953."

Bingham sipped his beer and listened. Phil had his own way of getting to the point and time was on their side.

"He was intense, you see – highly strung, as they say. He didn't like getting things wrong or cuttin' corners. You can be too … exact, sometimes."

"You mean he didn't fake the results?"

"That's exactly what I mean. Sometimes you can put yourself to a lot of trouble by being too punctilious."

Bingham didn't argue, although he felt himself to be on Robert's side. Phil probably wasn't too 'punctilious' about the exactness of his tax returns. Bingham wasn't sure what his friend did for a living. He'd never had a regular job but never claimed benefits. How he made ends meet was probably his own business, but Bingham didn't expect him to declare the five hundred pounds residing in the pocket of his camouflage trousers.

"Was that the only occasion on which you saw Robert?"

"Oh no! He never failed to come and say hello, even after he'd gone to university. He'd always come over and take an interest in what I was growing, and in the bees … He brought that friend with him once or twice."

Bingham noticed the pause and the expression twitching across Phil's face.

"Alan Vernon was this?"

"That was his name."

"Go on."

"I didn't like him. He was a queer."

"Queer?"

"You know."

"You mean gay?"

"Yes – if you like to use that word. Queer as a coot he was – a Nancy boy."

There was no point in Bingham contesting the use of a word that had become obsolete, not to say derogatory; Phil's children might one day catch up with the modern world, but it was unlikely their father would be with them.

"Are you saying that you think Robert was a homosexual?"

"No – far from it! What I didn't like was the influence the other one might have over him."

"Robert was impressionable?"

"Yes, and wound up, as I say. But a nice boy – you wouldn't want to see him come to harm."

They sat in silence after Phil had shared his thoughts, opening another beer each and listening to Britten's *A Charm of Lullabies*. Bingham wondered whether Phil realised that the man who composed the music had shown the world it was possible for a homosexual couple to live together, decently.

When *The Nurse's Song* ended, Bingham made his way to Bob's Farm, following the footpath that wound across and around fields from the village to his home. It was only when he reached the back door and the dogs ran to greet him that he realised he'd left Lina at the fair and still had the church treasurer's bag with its five hundred pounds in his pocket.

Chapter Two
THE POLITICIAN

Bingham normally enjoyed the train journey from Ipswich to London: at just over the hour, it gave him time to read the 'i' or have a short doze before he arrived to navigate his way across the Tube system.

Lina had seen him off at the station and he was to spend a few days with his daughter Cecilia, one of the twins, who was named after the Italian opera singer, a favourite of Lina's but whose style Bingham found lavish, not to say extravagant.

His telephone conversation the previous evening with Simon Brockie, the ex-Detective Chief Inspector who was an old friend, had failed to unsettle him despite Brockie's disinclination to discuss the case of Robert Courtney and his advice to "steer clear of this one, George".

He was nicely settled into his seat in the quiet coach, glasses on and hearing aid off, when the man who sat across the table opposite to him spoke. Bingham hadn't wanted a table seat since he objected to sitting where louts had rested their dirty shoes, but there had been no alternative, the train being full. It was, therefore, with both annoyance and reluctance that he raised his eyes.

He vaguely recognised the speaker – a large, heavy-faced man with a mass of white hair; he thought he might have seen him on local television or as the face above a newspaper column. He was left in no doubt when the man announced in a voice that boomed along the carriage.

"Sandy Malcolm – I contribute this and that to the local newspapers. You are George Bingham, aren't you – the man who got caught up in that business with the girl who was abducted? What was her name?"

If the journalist had forgotten, Bingham couldn't see the point in reminding him. Besides, he didn't want the girl's name broadcast, loudspeaker-wise, throughout the train. At the time, Natalie Beddoes's plight had been handled sensitively by the local media, and Bingham saw no reason for that to change now.

He looked the man up and down, wondering whether to move or point out that this was coach B and there seemed no point in banning mobile phones and musical laptops if people were going to talk at the tops of their voices.

Sandy Malcolm leaned forward, arms spread and stretched across the table towards Bingham, completely ignoring the fact that he was invading the space of the other people sitting next to them, a married couple who, forsaking the offerings of Upper Crust – a favourite of Bingham's when catching an early train – were sharing out a breakfast they'd brought from home.

"You are George Bingham?" repeated the journalist, his eyes widening and bearing down on the man he imagined might be his informant.

Bingham smiled and pulled his hearing aid box from his pocket.

"Ah – you're deaf!" shouted Sandy Malcolm.

"Hard of hearing," replied Bingham as he fixed one aid into his left year, "Claiming to be completely deaf would be unfair on those who are. It is a real affliction and socially debilitating in a talkative world. Oh – and there's no need to shout. It doesn't help. Diction is the thing – clear diction and distinctive phrasing on the lips. Background noise is also the very devil, which is why I like the quiet coach."

"Weren't you involved in that recent business with those gangsters, too? You're not after another missing person, are you – not that young devil who has run off with a quarter of a million?"

His voice had lost none of its booming quality as he pursued Bingham in true newshound fashion. The breakfast couple looked at each other and then at Bingham, annoyed at the volume of the journalist's voice but curious to discover whether Bingham was indeed the man Sandy Malcolm assumed him to be.

"As I said, there's no need to shout. Yes, I'm George Bingham ... "

A large hand outstretched itself across the table, gripped Bingham's responsive one and shook it vigorously.

"Pleased to meet you. My God, I've got to say I admire your guts. How's the shoulder?"

"It's fine. Thank you," replied Bingham, marvelling at the man's sudden recall.

"So, you're after this young, Whitehall chap now, are you? I must say he's got a nerve. How the devil does he expect to get away with it? The police will have him by the heels eventually. How come you're involved?"

Bingham didn't want to hand this man a story but was unsure how to sidestep his persistence. The truth

– that he had been asked to find Robert Courtney by Robert's mother – would unleash men and women like the one sitting opposite him at the widow's throat; a lie wasn't on the cards, if only out of consideration for Lina's feelings about lying of any kind.

"How do we know that the young man has absconded with the money?"

"It was in all the papers a couple of months ago."

"But that's all we do know, isn't it? I don't believe there's been an official statement from his department either acknowledging or refuting the allegations."

Lina, who was good at that sort of thing, had done Bingham's homework for him, sifting across the internet through newspaper items about Robert's disappearance.

"I think you'll find the allegations stand up to inspection."

"But they are allegations."

"Allegations supported by a reputable source or sources."

"You mean a 'leak'?

"If you like."

"Leaks allow liars to pursue their trade, since they're never called to account."

"Why would anyone wish to cast aspersions against the young man? Besides, he has disappeared with the money and without trace."

"Disappeared – yes, but we don't know that he's absconded, least of all with the money."

"What are you driving at, Mr Bingham?"

"I'm not driving at anything: merely pointing out that we shouldn't jump to conclusions on the basis of claims made by an unnamed informer."

"It's happened before, you know. Remember John Stonehouse? Left his clothes on a beach in Miami where they thought he either drowned or was eaten by a shark, while all the time he was living it up in Oz with his mistress and shifting his money from bank to bank."

Bingham cast his mind back, recalling how attractive Sheila Buckley, the mistress who became the wife, had been and how the papers had presented the case, harping on the infidelity and the mutual subterfuge. But Stonehouse had been a very intelligent man who had planned his disappearance carefully, adopting various identities to mask his travels. He was a man approaching fifty escaping from a series of failed business enterprises, and not a young man, inexperienced in the ways of the world and on the verge of a new career.

It was always the same with newspapers: they trawled up apparently similar cases from the past, forging links that did not exist, confusing a public hungry for scandal. Sandy Malcolm knew nothing. Bingham was sure of the fact. An old dog hungry for a fresh bone but who hadn't the teeth to do it justice.

"If you'll excuse me," he said, collecting his newspaper and glasses from the table.

He left the quiet coach, seeking somewhere he could read in peace.

From Liverpool Street station, Bingham caught the Central Line underground train to Holborn. He knew the area quite well for someone who stayed in London as infrequently as possible: in Red Lion Street there was a Premier Inn where he and Lina spent the night if they ever needed to stay after a visit to the theatre or concert hall, both preferring the freedom this gave them from relying on their daughters.

It was where Robert Courtney had his flat at £888 per calendar month, and to Bingham's delight was not far from Red Lion Square.

It was a little after eleven o'clock and time for coffee, which he intended to enjoy at the Café Gigi. The proprietress smiled, recognising him as the man who always ordered eggs royale whenever he and his wife came in for breakfast. He smiled back, ordered a croissant to go with his black coffee and sat by the window.

It was a warm morning, not to say muggy, and the promise of rain hung in the air. Bingham wished the sky would deliver its promise, although not necessarily while he searched for Robert's flat.

Once refreshed and on his way, Bingham found the flat easily; it was one situated in a purpose-built block. Each flat had its own balcony that looked out over a small park. He had the key to the actual flat but not the code to the security console by the door; he'd overlooked the need to get into the building but assumed someone might soon emerge.

He waited, and eventually a workman appeared carrying a ladder. Bingham supposed him to be undertaking maintenance work and explained his predicament.

"Mm – can I see your key?"

Bingham obliged, pulling Robert's key from his wallet.

"Right. It looks OK and so do you; otherwise, you'd be on your way by now, squire. Do you hear me? These blocks are secure premises and they're not secure for nothing: there're funny buggers round here."

"Are you from Suffolk?"

"What makes you ask?" replied the man, his eyes widening in a mixture of suspicion and surprise.

"Suffolk is the only place I've ever heard the expression 'funny buggers' used."

"Are you from there?"

"I live near Ipswich, now, but originally I'm from the Midlands."

"I was born in Woodbridge; I came down here for the work. Pleased to meet you. I'm Rob Saunders."

"Did you ever come across the young man I'm looking for – Robert Courtney?"

"Why'd you ask?"

"You're both from the same county. It forms a bond, doesn't it?"

"I suppose it does," replied Rob Saunders, looking Bingham up and down, "You're not a copper, are you? No, of course you're not. I'd have spotted that a mile off. Yeah, we passed the time of day. He was always polite. Not all of them will speak to a workman, but he never failed to say hello. Are you a friend of his?"

"I know his mother. We live in the same village."

"Right … Well, you can tell his mum from me that her boy is innocent. There's no way a lad like him would steal anything, let alone a quarter of a million, and there's no way a lad like him would run off."

"Say that again."

"There's no way a lad like him would run off, knowing he was innocent."

It was that moment again. Bingham had experienced it twice before: the first time when talking to the neighbour of Natalie Beddoes's mother and the second when listening to the gardener's wife in Guaro del Mar.

"Are you all right, squire?"

"Yes, yes thank you. I'd better let you get on. Thanks for your faith in Robert. I'll take a look at his flat."

He held the door while Rob Saunders walked through, the ladder swaying on his right shoulder. The maintenance man acknowledged the assistance and made his way to the basement, while Bingham climbed three flights of stairs to Robert Courtney's flat, where he was surprised to find a young man sitting, his legs splayed wide, in the central lounge.

"Good morning. I'm George Bingham. You must be Robert's flatmate."

"One of them: four of us share this flat. What do you want? Where did you get the key?"

Bingham smiled. He recognised the Suffolk accent, modified only slightly by the London twang that the young man probably assumed for social purposes.

"You're John Hunt, aren't you – the measurer of the speed of snails on various surfaces?"

"Who told you that? Did you know Robert?"

"No, not really: although I must have come across him on occasions. He was at school with my son, Ben."

"Ben Bingham?"

"Yes."

"He became a chemist, didn't he?"

"Yes, he works at John Innes in Norwich."

John Hunt, suddenly aware of his rudeness, leapt from the settee on which he'd been sprawled and shook Bingham's hand.

"Who told you about the snails? Mr Bassett?"

"Yes."

"It was fun that autumn. We spent hours on his allotment and whenever his wife knew we were going she sent over scones to have with our coffee. Well, Mr Bassett had coffee. We had a fizzy drink."

"Maureen, Phil's wife, likes cooking."

Suddenly, Bingham was back in the village, sitting with Phil by the pot-bellied stove enjoying Maureen Bassett's fruit scones while Phil brewed them a cup of black Yirgacheffe. He was struck by the unreality of being where he stood. Did all roads lead to Suffolk?

"Have you come to take back Robert's things?"

"No, I've come to look over his room."

"Why?"

"I'm looking for him. I need ..."

"... a lead?"

"A feeling of what he was like, of what he might think or do, of how he might behave. I take it you've no idea where he might be?"

"With respect, Mr Bingham, I don't know who you really are, and I am Robert's friend."

"Have you any idea where he might be hiding? Is there anyone you know who might have helped him?"

"No."

"Why are you sharing a flat together?"

"We're old friends. I got him the flat. I work for an estate agent around the corner in High Holborn."

"Why are you here at this time of day?"

"It's my lunch hour. I took it early because I've got to show a client round an apartment this afternoon."

"How come you work in London?"

"I like London. I moved down here from university. I wasn't going back to Ipswich."

"Who else shares this flat?"

"A couple of guys who work somewhere in the City; they're both in finance of one sort or another."

"Do you socialise together?"

"Occasionally we have a drink at one of the locals – the Red Lion, Princess Louise, Shakespeare's Head. These guys have got nothing to do with Robert if that's what you're thinking."

"Is one of them called Alan Vernon?"

"Him? No! You don't think he'd live here, do you? I expect his Daddy's bought him a place up West. Alan Vernon is what you might call a natural civil servant – born and bred to the role, unlike Robert who had to work for what he's achieved."

"What didn't you like about Alan Vernon?"

"He was aloof. Westminster – Eton – Oxford: the straight path to natural government, no additional effort required."

Bingham was averse to prejudice of any kind. Children couldn't help being privileged, and few adults would reject its advantages outright. It was the system that needed changing, not the people it produced.

"They'd been to university together, hadn't they? Were they very friendly?"

"What do you mean?"

"It's a straightforward question."

"Not in the way you're implying."

"I'm implying nothing."

"They worked together and sometimes they'd go to the theatre or a concert. Robert didn't really discover the theatre until he came to London, and he was fascinated."

"There's no chance he was being blackmailed is there?"

"No! You're on the wrong track, Mr Bingham."

"I'm on no track at all. I'm just wondering why Robert might have been tempted to take that money – if he did."

"He didn't."

"When did you last see him?"

"The day he ran away. He came home here, bundled a few things together and shot off. He didn't say anything except not to believe what I might read in the papers."

"What day was this?"

"Uh, I'm not sure. Oh yes, it was a Monday."

"What makes you so certain?"

"He had a *Big Issue* with him. He always bought his copy on a Monday."

"What time was this?"

"Midday – same as today and I was here for the same reason."

"Was his room searched?"

"You're not kidding. They went over that with a fine-tooth comb."

"Who did the search?"

"The local police. They were very good: they left everything just as they found it. They even returned his computer when they'd finished examining it … Look, Mr Bingham, it's been a pleasure, as they say, but I must go."

"Of course, John. Thanks for your help. If anything occurs to you, give me a ring. This is my number."

Bingham handed the young man a strip of paper he kept in his wallet so that he would remember his own mobile phone number. They shook hands, the door closed behind John Hunt and Bingham was alone in Robert Courtney's flat.

Robert's room was exactly as Bingham had imagined it: immaculate, even in the young man's absence. It was lighter and larger than the one at his home in Northfield.

The bed, a double one, was place firmly against the wall, leaving plenty of space in the centre of the room, and the desk was under the window where it would receive more light. On the desk was a pile of unopened letters. Most of them seemed like circulars or bills; one or two were of an official nature but none were personal. Bingham turned them over in his hands for a while and then replaced them carefully.

This time, Robert had a small wardrobe and an easy, cane chair. There was a mirror on the wall. The room was clean and fresh. Everything was in its place: socks and underpants in their respective drawers, as were Robert Courtney's shaving gear and deodorants. The small bookshelf contained nothing on economics; instead, there were several biographies of composers and playwrights. After the hard slog of qualifying for university and then obtaining his first-class honours degree, it appeared that Mabel Courtney's son left his work at the office and was in the business of expanding his social life.

After half-an hour of searching, Bingham had learned nothing. Robert Courtney was as far away as ever, and the afternoon spread before Bingham. He thought lunch might be appropriate – a small one, since Cecilia was likely to cook a dinner – and then he might wander to Whitehall where, it seemed, Robert's career started and his troubles began.

J D Wetherspoon provided his lunch at Penderel's Oak on High Holborn. Bingham was a fan of Wetherspoon: he'd seen the company restore broken-down premises and rescue dying pubs, restoring them to their former selves, always alert to the original purpose of the building however long dead that purpose might be.

He found a corner seat so that he could sit with his back to the wall, a strategy that always cut out the background noise, from where he could think quietly and watch the world go by while he enjoyed one of Wetherspoon's new dishes, a Mediterranean vegetable lasagne, which he washed down with a pint of Guardsman. At £7.49 for both the meal and the drink who could grumble?

It was 3 o'clock before Bingham left the public house. He wasn't sure why and wondered whether he'd dozed off after his lunch. He just hoped he hadn't snored. He felt it was too late, now, to venture to Whitehall. He needed a rest and decided to go straight to his daughter's flat in Bloomsbury.

He stood outside for a while admiring the long flow of terraced houses fronted by the elegant railings from which steps led down to the basements. The month's rent of any one of the many flats these houses had become would swallow up more than the pension he'd earned working as a teacher for forty years, and he wondered how Cecilia managed; he couldn't believe the salary of a politician's secretary covered the cost. Was it the father of her child, Bruno, who helped to foot the bill or her current boss, a Labour MP representing a Midlands' constituency?

Bingham wondered, but not too deeply. It had always been his policy, not one shared entirely by Lina, never to poke his nose into his children's business. Both girls had been on the wild side, and Cecilia had succumbed to the charms of a German law student while on holiday in Munich when she was nineteen years old – little more than a child in Bingham's eyes. Succumbed wasn't the word, perhaps, and unfair on the charmer: Cecilia had enjoyed the charms of the young man.

Bingham hadn't disliked him, although he hadn't approved of both young people deciding that marriage between them was not an option; Bingham was aware of a puritanical streak running through him, which he put down to his Protestant upbringing. He and Lina had looked after Bruno while Cecilia was at university, something upon which they'd insisted, and so he knew his grandson very well. It was no surprise then that the boy ran out to meet him.

"Grandad!"

"Bruno!"

The boy flung his arms around his grandfather and held him for a moment before looking up at him.

"How are the bees?"

"Enjoying their autumn feed and about to appreciate a well-earned rest."

The flat had been let unfurnished and Cecilia with Bruno roamed antique and junk shops looking for bargains; the flat reflected her searches, and Bingham eased himself into an English bergere chair his daughter had bought as a bargain and restored.

"Mum will be home soon. I'm always in first."

"I've got something for you," said Bingham, a quiet smile crossing his face at the excitement in the boy's eyes. "We had our autumn fair at the weekend, and I sold three hundred jars of honey at five pound a jar. Here's your share of the rewards."

Bingham handed the boy twenty-five ten-pound notes and laughed at the frown on his grandson's face.

"If it hadn't been for you and Phil, I'd never have gathered in the honey. I gave him five hundred pounds and split our share between us."

"And the other five hundred is for the church?"

"Yes."

"Thank you, grandad. Are you sure?"

"Positive – the labourer is worthy of his hire."

"Mum takes me every Sunday morning to Mass, you know, grandad."

The question wasn't as much out of the blue as it sounded. His grandson had raised the matter before as they tended the bees, and for the boy it was becoming an issue.

"Do you enjoy it?"

"It's all right, but I'm not sure I believe it all. Do you?"

"I'd rather not answer that question, Bruno."

"Why?"

"It's a question that deserves more than a snap answer. All I will say is this," replied Bingham, pausing for a moment, "at the end of the day, any decision anyone comes to about their religious beliefs – or anything else of importance, for that matter – is down to the individual conscience. One of your popes said that – John Paul the First – and it's true."

"Are Pippa and Ben and George all right?"

Bingham laughed and ruffled the boy's hair. It was so typical of childhood that one minute his mind could be occupied with matters that had toppled nations and the next ask about the pet dogs.

"Take me for a walk in the park," said Bingham.

By the time they returned, the smell of cooking was coming from the kitchen and it wasn't long before they settled down to a carrot pesto bake. They were joined at the table by Dan Jessop, Cecilia's employer, who she had invited for her father's benefit.

When Bruno had excused himself to go to bed, it was Dan Jessop who opened the conversation.

"I understand from Cecilia that you're looking for Robert Courtney, George?"

"Yes. His mother believes it's in his best interests to give himself up and rely on our police officers to clear his name."

"Do you think that's likely to happen – the police clearing his name, I mean?"

"I don't share the media-led scepticism about the integrity of our police force, Dan. No doubt there are bent pennies among them, but most of our coppers are people like you and me – people who just want to help create a decent society, free of the toe-rags."

"But this is a Whitehall matter, George, and it's unlikely to be investigated by your everyday policeman ..."

"... or woman," cut in Cecilia.

"I stand corrected, but can we just accept the term 'policeman' as applying to both sexes? We can't have a policeperson."

"We could just say police officer, Dan," replied Cecilia, and Bingham wondered what she was like as a colleague.

"The police *officer* likely to be involved would be from Special Branch ..."

"Special Branch," interrupted Bingham, "I thought they were part of MI5 these days or the Anti-Terrorist Branch? What's it called?"

"All police forces have their Special Branch, and the Metropolitan Anti-Terrorist Branch is called SO13," replied Dan Jessop. "The role of Special Branch falls between that of MI5, the Security Service, and that of SO13. MI5 officers are not authorised to perform arrests, and so this function is delegated to the Special Branch. What is more, the Special Branch of the Metropolitan Police has recently been merged with SO13 to form SO15 or, if you prefer it, Counter Terrorism Command."

Bingham, already tired from a long day, was beginning to lose interest and this must have been apparent from the expression on his face because Dan Jessop's mocking tone suddenly changed.

"What we've just been saying illustrates the point I am here to make, George. It's confusing, isn't it, and it's meant to be. Confusion keeps the plebs at bay: what you can't get your head round, you can't criticise effectively. And nowhere is that maxim believed more earnestly than in Whitehall, where you will be up against the Civil Service."

"Let's just clear one thing aside. You're not suggesting that Robert Courtney is a spy or a terrorist, are you?"

"Who knows? He absconded with a quarter of a million pounds having spent his university days at Oxford. Both of our senior universities have produced some very effective spies over the years, and who is to say that your young man isn't one of them. He may have been 'turned', as the expression goes, during his student days, when idealistic young men are very vulnerable, and left in a hurry if he thought he'd been discovered."

"No," replied Bingham, "no, no and no."

"It could be the case, Dad."

Bingham threw a glance at his daughter and rose from the chair he'd commandeered as his own. He walked to the window. Night was falling and the street was quiet. The late, hot summer had denuded the few pavement-planted trees of their leaves and the only colour in the dusk was that of a red pillar box.

"You'll need to understand what you're up against if you pursue this matter," said Dan Jessop, speaking to Bingham's back.

"I'm listening," replied Bingham, returning to his chair and accepting, but not drinking, the whisky Cecilia placed in his hand.

"The key point to grasp is that the Civil Service protects its own …"

Bingham thought he could be excused for thinking that it hadn't protected Robert Courtney but remained silent; he pondered only on the idea that perhaps Robert wasn't senior enough to be favoured.

"… by the simple strategy," continued Dan Jessop, "of believing that Whitehall knows best and everyone else is ignorant of the real facts or out to make trouble. You will have already gathered that Robert's department has issued no official allegations against him, but neither have they refuted those made by the media. It puts them in a very strong position whatever the outcome. They have either leaked lies about Robert Courtney for reasons of their own or decided that it is in their interest not to deny lies written by others."

"Or both," said Cecilia.

"I find my mathematical equations easier to understand."

"Dad, let's suppose that Robert Courtney had in some way or other, behaved badly, disgraced himself – call it what you will. What would you do?"

"Sack him if what he did was bad enough."

"Exactly – but the Whitehall mandarins wouldn't see it in the same way. They would have appointed him in the first place, and to find fault in him would be to find fault in them."

"You must have noticed," continued Dan Jessop, "that whenever an enquiry into some government cock-up has to be organised that it is led by the very same senior civil servants who were responsible for the cock-up in the first place. It's called the 'Whitehall Loop'. You need to read Tim Slessor's book, *Ministries of Deception*, on the subject."

"Perhaps you could buy it for me as a Christmas present, Cecilia?"

"I'll make a note of it, Dad," replied Cecilia, smiling at her father's sarcasm.

"You see, in that way their judgement, and therefore their fitness to run the country, can never be questioned. The Civil Service decides the rules that best suit them. They are accountable only to themselves."

"Put very, very simply you are telling me that their failure to respond to Robert's alleged actions is simply to avoid any embarrassment to themselves?"

"They may even have assisted his escape. Remember Kim Philby? Not only was he never brought to account when the security services had laid hands on him and begun an interrogation, but he was also allowed to escape."

Bingham couldn't sleep that night; several times he got up and made himself a cup of tea. He didn't doubt that what his daughter and her boss were saying was true and may well have some bearing on Robert Courtney's flight; what he couldn't believe was that Robert Courtney, the boy who had measured the relative speed of snails on a variety of surfaces only a few years before, could be a spy or a terrorist – or, indeed, a criminal of any sort.

Chapter Three

THE COLLEAGUE

Armed with the misgivings heaped upon him by his daughter and her boss, Bingham made his way to Whitehall, hoping to locate the department, deep within the bowels of the Treasury, responsible for employing Robert Courtney as a junior clerk; in particular, he wanted to find Alan Vernon – the friend who should be able to answer so many of the questions that had given Bingham his sleepless night.

Bingham was prepared to be over-awed by the Treasury, not so much by the civil servants who presided over its eminence in public life or the grandeur of the building itself but by its inaccessibility to people like him – the very people who enabled its existence through the regular payment of their taxes.

His acquaintance with Dan Jessop had secured him, at least, a visitor pass, something that raised a quaint smile on the face of the doorman (not uniformed in splendour as Bingham had expected but wearing a simple high-visibility body warmer) who ushered him forward to the reception desk. This was, to his surprise, modern in design and style. A young woman greeted him with a smile that filled the entrance hall. She wasted no time in assuring him that she would pass his request to Mr Vernon, but that Mr Vernon was likely to be busily engaged until, at least, his lunch hour. The young woman recommended that Bingham should acquaint himself with St James's Park, a delightful spot in which he might "hire a deck chair and watch the world go by".

In less than five minutes, with arrangements made that Mr Vernon would meet him at Inn the Park or, at the very least, telephone to say he was unable to do so, Bingham found himself standing on the pavement outside 1 House Guards Road with time on his hands and the doorman's laughter at the 'Inn' joke ringing in his ears.

He crossed the road, oblivious to the queue for Churchill's War Rooms, and stood watching the Treasury building from the park. A steady trickle of people made its way in and out the building, everyone contributing to its flow acknowledged by a broad smile from the doorman; some seemed intent on one purpose or another, some exited merely to stand and smoke on the pavement. Nearly all were dressed in an informality that surprised Bingham: he'd expected jackets and ties or smart dresses at the very least, if not striped suits for both men and women, rather than the open-necked shirts, causal trousers and miniskirts. He realised the world had moved on; he suddenly felt old.

Bingham wasn't used to time on his hands; if one thing irritated him above all other minor considerations it was killing time. Having dozed off in the Penderel Oak, he had wasted the previous afternoon and now an empty morning loomed before him. He'd eaten breakfast at Cecilia's and so the fact that one was probably served until 11am at Inn the Park held no attraction.

The park and its surrounds seemed cluttered with statues and memorials – Queen Victoria's, the Duke of

York's and King George V1's among them – but he'd never found such monuments appealing and wondered what King George, by all accounts a modest man and the person after whom Bingham had been named, would think if he could see himself looking down on the world from his plinth of Portland stone.

The park was crowded with people, tourists from all over the world and groups of schoolchildren mainly but also couples and individuals drawn by the wildlife and the peacefulness here in the centre of the country's capital city, some stretched out on the grass, others lounging in the many deck chairs mentioned by the receptionist. He wended his way through the throng, oblivious to the squirrels, ducks and geese that approached him for food as he was oblivious to the people, his mind on an impregnable building and a young man on the run.

It was another muggy day. The heat of the previous week had built to a point where only a good downfall could clear the air. Within half-an-hour of his time-killing perambulations, Bingham was soaked in sweat, his open collar sticking to his neck, his thick, wavy hair congealing against his scalp, his socks swelling inside his shoes. He wasn't a man to become irritated easily, but he felt that even the weather seemed to be conspiring against him.

Wandering round the park, he realised how powerless he was to influence events. Somehow or other he had to gain access to the Treasury – if not the building then to those people who worked in its various departments. Central to Robert Courtney's dilemma there was a lie, but who was the liar or liars?

No one he'd spoken to had anything but good to say about Robert, even Phil Bassett, a natural sceptic, and the maintenance man, Rob Saunders, both of whom barely knew the young man. The only ones to cast any doubt had been Sandy Malcolm, the local journalist, and his own daughter and her boss, none of whom had met him.

Nevertheless, Bingham, despite what he'd said the previous evening, was for keeping an open mind: he'd known young men, pushed to the edge for whatever reason, do foolish things, often on the spur of the moment, always believing they could put matters right before their transgressions had been discovered.

But who had leaked the story, true or false, to the newspapers – and why? It was obvious, even to the most generous mind, that government departments told lies. The phrase 'economical with the truth' was firmly embedded in the public consciousness since Robert Armstrong had used it at the time of the *Spycatcher* trial to defend statements he'd made in a letter; and, likewise, Alan Clarke, defended himself with a similar phrase 'economical with the actualite' when cross-examined over arms deals to Iraq. Both men had brought the integrity of government into disrepute, a stain on its character that had become permanent.

While Bingham accepted that lies were told and that it was likely government departments would rather lie than be seen to be incompetent, he did not believe that there was necessarily an open conspiracy to deceive the public; he could not visualise groups of civil servants and politicians sitting around a table discussing how they might lie their way out of the latest cock-up. It was far more likely to be a kind of camaraderie whereby the bureaucrats involved simply understood what was expected of them and toed the line, realising that spilling the beans would be an embarrassment for all concerned. Bingham could see the smiles of conspiracy on the faces of those concerned.

What he couldn't see was why or where any lie might have started in the first place. Robert Courtney was, presumably, a very junior clerk in the Treasury. Bingham was unsure whether he served a minister or another civil servant, minor or senior. Why would anyone lie about someone who would surely be considered a relatively unimportant clerk? Besides, there was the fact that the money had appeared in Robert's bank account. Or had it? No one had shown him the actual account.

There was also the fact that he had run away, an act uncharacteristic of him as far as those who knew him were concerned. And what had he run away from: the police investigation, the shame, or the inevitable restrictions on his freedom to prove his innocence?

Of one thing Bingham was sure: there would be a wall of silence confronting him if ever he gained entrance to the Treasury. If he couldn't go to the Treasury, his only hope was that the Treasury would come to him, at lunch time, in the form of Alan Vernon. Perhaps that would be s start.

Bingham had been walking slowly, immersed in his thoughts. When he looked up, unsure of where he was, he found himself walking beneath some beech trees, his feet kicking through a rustle of early autumn leaves. He was outside the park and looking up he saw the statue of George V1 on the far side of The Mall. He realised he must have crossed the Blue Bridge and missed its spectacular views without appreciating either the beauty of the lake or his loss. He gazed at the figure on the plinth, a thoroughly decent man who'd insisted on staying in London with his family during the Blitz, a man who had been a boyhood hero of Bingham's, a man who represented a time when the integrity and selflessness of leadership was admired and taken for granted.

The thought bucked Bingham up: perhaps his morning hadn't been wasted after all. He'd failed to wonder at the beauty of St James's Park, but he had cleared his head and settled his purpose. He saw no light at the end of the tunnel, but he did, at least, see the tunnel. Perhaps labyrinth might be a better word, he thought, as he made his way towards Inn the Park. It was too early for lunch, but he might enjoy a late coffee.

The girl at the reception desk who the information notice told Bingham to consult was less than helpful, directing him to the self-service food counter when all he wanted was a coffee and to nowhere in particular when he asked the way to a seat on the roof. It was only later he realised that she was a foreigner, holding down a job and struggling to be understood in a second language. Bingham wondered how he might fare in a country where the language and the culture were a mystery to him and made a quiet promise that he'd leave her a decent tip if she happened to serve them when Alan Vernon arrived.

When he did, Bingham recognised the young man at once from Mabel Courtney's description of him as 'aloof' and Phil Bassett's as 'queer', although Bingham jumped to no conclusions about the accuracy of either comment. Certainly, Alan Vernon possessed the distinctive walk Bingham had noticed in many of the gay young men he worked with in the world of amateur theatre and he, also, had a habit of looking down his nose at passers-by; but these characteristics might simply be a matter of taste, upbringing or a natural lack of confidence. The thing that distinguished Alan Vernon from all others in the park to Bingham, as he watched him approach from the rooftop, was his smart suit, pinstriped and bespoke.

They were refused a seat on the terrace because they hadn't booked, but the young woman found them one in the restaurant, tucked in by a pillar where there were hangers for their jackets and where Bingham could sit comfortably cushioned with his back to a screen; although the restaurant was only just filling up and noise levels were low, he was aware that hearing would be a problem, speaking as they were bound to do in low voices.

"I'm pleased you got in touch with me, George. I understand from Inaya that you want to talk about Robert."

Bingham smiled to himself. Few people who were strangers to him used his Christian name on first acquaintance; here was one who did and who also expected him to know that Inaya was the young receptionist. Alan Vernon didn't bat an eyelid at Bingham's smile: a lack of confidence obviously wasn't an issue.

Alan Vernon ordered the dish of the day, a whole mackerel with a fennel and grapefruit salad, while Bingham settled for organic spelt risotto with peas, lemon, courgettes and Berkeswell cheese.

"I see you're a vegetarian, George. I've thought about it, but I don't seem to get around to doing anything. You know how it is. Isn't it awful about Robert? I really ought to go and see his mother, but it's a question of time. I assume it was Mabel who gave you my name. He was such a fool to run as he did. I can't understand it. The whole thing is so unlike Robert. Those of us at the Treasury who knew him just cannot believe what's happening."

"You knew him well?" asked Bingham, keen to stem Alan Vernon's flow, which threatened to develop into a stream of consciousness.

"We were at Oxford together. He was brighter them me, of course. Robert was brighter than everyone. But he was well-liked. You couldn't dislike Robert," replied Alan, adding "He had his whole future in front of him."

"You were good friends?"

"He and I enjoyed the theatre and classical concerts and we went together."

"Did he have any other close friends?"

"There were a few, I believe."

"Would you have any idea of where they are now?"

"Not really. It's another world, isn't it – university? Once those years have gone, you move on – new friends, new experiences."

There was a certain teasing quality in Alan Vernon's tone that irritated Bingham. It wasn't so much he felt the young man wanted to hold back: more, that he was the possessor of knowledge he required Bingham to lever from him.

"Had Robert established a social circle here in London?"

"There was his friend at the flat – the estate agent. I think they had a drink together now and then."

"Do you know any of them?"

"They're not really my cup of tea, are they?"

"Does he have a girlfriend?"

"Do you know your generation always makes me laugh? My parents are just the same – find a girlfriend, settle down and be happy! The nearest Robert's got to a girlfriend since he arrived in London is the girl who he buys *The Big Issue* off every Monday morning outside Holborn underground station – some migrant or other," replied Alan Vernon rather peevishly, adding by way of lightening his disgruntlement, "He's got to know her well. He talks about her a lot. Perhaps she can tell you where he is."

"How close was your friendship with Robert?"

Alan Vernon paused (his knife in the process of scraping flesh from the tail of the mackerel) and looked Bingham up and down. Mabel Courtney's description returned to Bingham as the young man watched him.

"It was very close considering our different *sexual orientation*. That's the phrase, isn't it, George?"

Bingham realised he was being corrected, although he was unsure why he'd caused offence. Alan placed the knife and fork on his plate, took a sip of the Trebbiano he'd ordered to go with the fish and focussed his eyes on Bingham in a stare that was quiet and unflinching. He didn't speak, and Bingham realised this was intentional. Bingham returned the gaze, aware he was being assessed as to his worthiness for the conversation to continue.

"You mustn't suppose all gay people have an interest in *cruising*, George. Many of us enjoy the company of people like you. One of our problems is that people like you, especially young men like you, aren't keen to be seen in the company of a gay man in case other people get the *wrong idea*. Robert wasn't like that."

His little homily over, Alan Vernon returned his attention to the mackerel and salad, attempting to spear a piece of grapefruit to accompany the fish to his mouth. Bingham was aware that the young man had delivered similar speeches before, so precise was his stress on certain words and phrases.

"Did you tend to move in the same social circles at Oxford?"

"Robert was well-liked by everyone. We mixed and mingled, as you might say."

"Did he have girlfriends?"

"You are persistent, George."

"I'm trying to establish Robert's circle of friends. If he's in hiding, it must be somewhere, and it might be with a friend or with the help of a friend. From what Mabel Courtney told me, you were the only one he took home."

"Yes, very well. We were close but not in the way people often suppose. Robert was not 'limp in the left wrist', as Mr Caine so elegantly puts it. He had girlfriends as I had boyfriends but none of them lasted the course. We were both, shall we say, *particular*? Robert never found what he was after and neither did I."

"Was it a coincidence that you both ended up in the Treasury?"

"For me it was a natural progression: home, school, university, Civil Service. I liked Robert and suggested he might find a real role for himself as a statistician or even an actuary. I didn't want him to return to Ipswich and sink without trace into some insurance company. I knew the Civil Service would treat someone of his abilities with respect, and that he'd have a chance to shape the nation's future. The Civil Service isn't the closed club – a branch of the old boy network – that the public so often supposes. As a graduate, Robert would be offered a role as a policy adviser and would be expected to move around the various departments within the Treasury. It would open up many career paths for him."

Bingham listened to the young man getting hot under the collar; the initial impression he'd given of foppishness had disappeared completely. There was pique within the anger, and Bingham wondered whether he might know more than he was saying. Was it simply 'a question of time' preventing him from visiting Robert's mother or was it more likely to be a matter of expediency?

The lunch hour was vanishing quickly, Alan Vernon suddenly seemed to be a young man who wouldn't return late for work in the afternoon and Bingham was no nearer finding Robert Courtney.

"Robert's mother is keen he should hand himself in to the authorities. It would be better for me to find him first."

"I understand, George."

"What was the attitude at the Treasury towards his relationship with you?"

"Why should the Treasury adopt any particular attitude? This is the twenty first century."

"Surely they keep an eye on their young recruits?"

"It wouldn't be considered politically correct if they did, George. I cannot say that either Robert or I have been aware of any particular surveillance."

His tone had returned to its light-hearted mode; it was one with which he was most comfortable.

Bingham took a long drink from his pint of Saxon lager and waited. He had decided Alan Vernon enjoyed conversation in all its complexities, and that it was better that he should draw the conclusions. Eventually, after a few more carefully selected mouthfuls, he said:

"Do you think Robert was involved in some sort of scandal? Even these days, there must be those people who would see the opportunity for blackmail."

"I've been abused, of course. That still goes on – the spiteful remark as you leave the pub, the laughter behind your back, people moving aside when you pass by, a group of them snatching your bag – but never blackmail."

"Do you think he took the money?"

"No, I don't"

"So why has he run away?"

"I don't know, and I must say I find it irritating. Robert wasn't any more likely to abscond than he was to be bothered by blackmail – not that I believe he was blackmailed. Robert had courage. He stood by a friend."

"He stood by you?"

"Yes."

"When they tried to snatch your bag?"

It wasn't a shot in the dark by Bingham: he'd noticed the catch in Alan Vernon's voice when he mentioned the bag snatching. It wasn't a standard grievance; it was a memory.

"I'd been returning to college one evening with a bag of food we'd bought. Nothing much: some wine and some cheese and biscuits. There was a group of us, but I went ahead to lay out the spread in my room. The others were still at the club and Robert must have left soon after me. He had a girl with him. As I passed this pub, a group of drunks kicked the bag out of my hand. The food went all over the cobblestones. Robert must have seen them. I heard the girl scream and then saw him running towards me shouting. The drunks went back into the pub."

"There's no shame in tears, Alan."

"I was brought up not to cry," replied the young man, taking a handkerchief from his trouser pocket and dabbing at his eyes.

"So were we all, but life teaches a different lesson. Often it only takes something small, something apparently insignificant, to tip someone over the edge. The memory is still painful, is it, son?"

"Robert wouldn't let the others see me. He steered me to my room and set the food up in his – or his girl did."

"Is that what the tears were for – the memory?"

"What do you mean?"

"It happened several years ago."

Alan Vernon stared at Bingham, his eyes still moist and full of anger.

"What happened on the morning Robert ran away?"

"I didn't work in his department. None of us knew until later."

"When you read it in the papers?"

"Yes."

"Did he phone you?"

"Why would he?"

"Did he phone you?"

"No."

"Was it a letter?"

"He just said to trust him, that he wasn't guilty and that he'd ..."

"He'd what?"

"Nothing ... He'd be in touch."

"But he hasn't been?"

"No."

"What's the word going around the Treasury?"

"We're not encouraged to talk about it."

"At work?"

"Yes."

"But outside – on the social scene?"

"Look, George, I must go. It's been a longer than usual lunch hour but quite delightful. Thank you for the lunch ... Perhaps we'll meet again?"

"I'd like to see the letter. Same time, same place, tomorrow?"

"I may not be able to – it depends on my work commitments."

"Then, let's exchange phone numbers so that we do not lose touch."

Ashen was the colour of the young man's face but Bingham held his eyes and he couldn't refuse – not decently, not if the man on the run was his friend. Bingham jotted down the number in his notebook. As Alan Vernon left, Bingham called after him:

"Give my regards to Sir Herbert."

This was a shot in the dark, played with the skills Bingham had acquired as an amateur actor: the ability not so much to lie as to create an artificial impression. The young man frowned, almost smiled and paled slightly – not so much in fear but in wonder. Unusually lost for words, Bingham thought, Alan Vernon left rapidly.

Through the window of the terrace, Bingham saw him walking along the pathway that led to Horse Guards Road, his place of work and his shelter. Had he the authority, had he been a police officer, Bingham would have "hauled him in". As Simon Brockie used to say, "I'd break him, George."

Bingham asked for the bill – £37.88 worth of nothing as far as any useful information was concerned – and noticed the 12.5% service charge. Bingham disliked such charges, preferring to tip for good service and foreseeing the day when the dreadful American system of auto-gratuities would become the norm and young people, knowing no better times, would stump up the money without question. He placed two twenty-pound notes under his wine glass next to the bill, deciding that was enough to keep his silent promise to tip the waitress, having thought poorly of her when he arrived.

Outside in the park, returning his hearing aids to their boxes because they were tickling his ears, Bingham suddenly found a packet of peanuts in his pocket. Bruno had given them to him to feed the squirrels but preoccupied as he was Bingham had noticed no squirrels.

Returning alongside the lake, making his way he wasn't sure where, Bingham remedied his oversight. One grey squirrel followed him along the top of the low metal fence, sniffed his hand, accepted the peanut and darted off, clutching the white shell between its forepaws. Another followed, and then another, drawn by the promise of food. As Bingham handed out the treats, several tourists gathered round him, snapping photographs, entranced by the trusting nature of the creatures and the delicacy with which they accepted the nuts.

Bingham wondered how many of them might be enjoying squirrel for dinner that evening. It was London's latest delicacy and available in the best restaurants. Bingham knew his mood was anything but jovial; he was feeling sour. It wasn't Alan Vernon's refusal to help that turned his stomach so much as the feeling he'd had when saying goodbye to Mabel Courtney – the feeling that this was an unpleasant business, which couldn't end happily.

Moreover, he was now feeling locked out, trapped in a world of dual standards, surrounded by the natural hypocrisy of ordinary lives.

Chapter Four

THE VENDOR

What made him approach the girl, Bingham was unsure; on a Wednesday afternoon, she might not even be selling her paper by the Underground station.

The mugginess in the air had intensified since lunch, and all he really wanted to do was doze off, comfortably, somewhere. A park bench would have done, but there was business needing his attention and there was that wretched conscience of his, something a colleague (lazy in the extreme, in Bingham's view) once described as "his Protestant work ethic" in tones of derision. A fair day's work for a fair day's pay had been a guiding light for Bingham; not that he was expecting any payment for this day's work – at least not in financial terms.

Hanging over him, together with the mugginess of the September day, was a feeling of heaviness brought on by a sense of despondency. This business couldn't end happily; his thought on leaving Mabel Courtney kept returning. It was intuition, of course: there was nothing logical about the idea. But then, he'd never been noted for his logical approach to any problem. Strange, perhaps, in a mathematician, although his university lecturers had always said it was his intuition that raised him above the average in his chosen subject.

Bingham caught the Underground train from Westminster, missed his stop at Embankment, having been flummoxed by a young woman offering him her seat, was assured by her that he would reach Holborn by carrying on to Monument where he could make his way to Bank and hence, via the Central Line, to Holborn. Two stiflingly hot trains and lots of walking later he found himself on the pavement outside Holborn Underground station.

The young woman was standing with her armful of *The Big Issue* several yards along High Holborn, offering her wares discreetly, not waylaying those who passed by – some with a nod and a smile but most turning to look across the road at nothing or no one in particular. Bingham usually bought his copy from a regular vendor in Ipswich, one who stood in the Buttermarket outside Waterstones; to other vendors he gave a smile, a "No thanks" or pointed to the copy in his coat pocket. Only once had he felt threatened, when a tall vendor accompanied by his bull terrier wondered whether Bingham wanted change from his five-pound note. Bingham did, and got it; he never used the vendor again.

The young woman (a generic term for Bingham's generation of men to describe any woman under sixty) was, indeed, young. Bingham guessed she couldn't have left her early twenties and might even be in her late teens. He smiled and bought a copy, telling her to keep the change from the three-pound coins he offered. She was dark-skinned and wide-eyed and wore the type of headscarf that covered her hair and ears and fell to her shoulders, hiding her neck but leaving her face open to the sun. He couldn't place her nationality and didn't like to ask. Somehow, these days, it was considered discourteous rather than a natural curiosity about a person's roots.

"Is this your pitch?"

"Yes," replied the girl with a smile.

"I'm not from round here," continued Bingham, keen to hold her in conversation, "I live in a little village to the north of Ipswich, where I usually buy my copy."

There was a faint flicker of recognition in the girl's eyes at the mention of Ipswich, and Bingham realised he'd hit at least one nail on the head.

"I'm down here for a few days visiting my daughter."

"Yes," replied the girl, whether because her grasp of the language was limited or because she didn't wish to be engaged in conversation Bingham was unsure.

"You must have your regular customers, like my vendor?"

"Yes, the same people often."

"Have you worked this pitch long?"

"Some time – a year or so."

"It's OK in the summer, I expect, but not so pleasant in winter?"

"Yes. I work from nine o'clock until four o'clock every day."

"Whatever the weather?"

"Yes, whatever the weather, but the summer is best," replied the girl with a smile.

Bingham could feel a tension building between them. It was difficult holding a conversation with someone who simply agreed with you, and he was aware that he was keeping her from her job. He didn't like to be persistent, but he needed this young woman's help.

"I expect they share their troubles with you?"

"They tell me their stories."

"And their troubles?"

"And their troubles."

"Everyone has a worry of some sort, and you listen."

"I am always polite. I say please and thank you. I was brought up to show respect."

"And you receive respect in return?"

"Mostly. Some people do not feel the same way, but there are always such people."

"Wherever you are in the world?"

"Yes," replied the girl, her face, which had lightened during their last exchange, falling, once again, into a troubled expression.

"I travelled a great deal when I was young, and I've found that people are much the same all over the world," urged Bingham, adding in an attempt to draw the girl out, "Do you enjoy talking with your customers?"

"Yes, of course, it helps my English."

"Your English is very good," replied Bingham, with a smile, "It's certainly superior to my Arabic."

Again, the startled expression appeared in the girl's eyes.

"You speak Arabic?"

"None at all. My travels did not include Arabic-speaking countries. I can only admire the way you have picked up a language foreign to you."

The girl's smile once more lit up her face at the compliment.

"I am from Syria," she said, in a moment of trust.

"A refugee?"

"Yes."

"Welcome to my country," replied Bingham, "I hope my people treat you well."

"I am hoping to make my home here."

"You have somewhere to live?"

"Yes, I share a small flat with some friends. *The Big Issue* helps me to pay my rent and my bills. I share with friends. We help each other out."

"Syrian friends?"

"Some are, but not all. We …"

Bingham waited, wondering whether the pause indicated a need to find the right word or whether the girl felt she was divulging too much to a stranger.

"We have a mixture pf people in the flats," she explained at last.

"Some who can help you with your English?"

"Yes: but there are the classes, too."

"Language classes?"

"Yes, they are very helpful."

Bingham felt he had gained at least a small measure of trust. Should he ask his question or lengthen their conversation almost unnaturally?

"I'm staying with my daughter, as I explained, but I'm in London to find the son of a friend of mine," he said after a pause during which the young woman sold two more of her papers. "He used to live round here but seems to have moved on. You wouldn't by any chance know him, would you? He might have been one of your customers."

Bingham lifted Robert's photograph from his pocket and showed the young woman. Her face fell yet again, and a vicious blend of anger and fear crossed her face, scarring the beauty of her eyes, lifting her mouth into an unspoken cry of rage. She turned abruptly and ran towards the Underground station, casting a warning look at Bingham as she did so; the look was also one of terror.

He wasn't sure whether the girl had run into Holborn Station or whether she'd simply made for one of the side streets off the main road. It didn't matter. He could hardly chase her through London. Bingham had almost expected the reaction: after all, where she came from there was no doubt a police force that kept its eye on the people – the bully boys of a dictatorship. He cursed himself quietly for being a fool, for ignoring the wisdom of his old age; but by the time he'd reached Penderel's Oak his mind was made up and he rang Lina.

Another day had passed by, his third in London, before they sat together over another pint for him in Penderel's Oak and a gin and tonic for her.

"I needed that," said Lina, having drained half the glass in one gulp, "It's been quite an adventure."

She had answered his call and arrived at Liverpool Street soon after lunch, having left Phil in charge of the animals. They ate at Carluccio's in Spitalfields, while Bingham detailed his request.

"You want me to just follow this young woman home?"

"Yes, please, Lina. I obviously can't, but I think she might know where Robert is hiding – if he's hiding. There was no point in you hurrying down because the young woman works her pitch until four o'clock. You can't miss her if you're around Holborn Underground station at that time."

"Don't you think the police would have found him by now if he was living there?"

"I don't say that he's living there – just that the young woman may know where he is or, at the very least, give us some clue."

Obligingly, Lina had arrived in High Holborn at three o'clock, wandered round aimlessly, keeping out of sight, for an hour and then followed the *Big Issue* vendor home.

"Do you know how far I've walked today, Bing?"

"No," replied Bingham, but sure that it was some distance.

"In this heat?"

"Go on."

"Five miles at least. It was six o'clock when we arrived at the young woman's flat. The Victoria Embankment was attractive enough, but then we turned north towards the Minories before walking the length of Whitechapel Road. Do you know how long Whitechapel Road is, Bing?"

"I've never thought about it, Lina."

"You would if you'd walked it. It's long enough to have earned me a day's shopping in London when you've finished. I think another gin might be in order."

Bingham obliged, and the young woman, perceiving him to have become a regular, offered to bring the gin to their table together with his "usual pint".

"You are OK, aren't you, Lina?"

"I am now. But I was just a sweating grease spot by the time we reached the girl's flat. I'm not young anymore, Bing. Following at that girl's pace was crippling. I don't think I had a dry stitch on me when we arrived in Mile End."

"You did well to cover five miles in two hours through the London crowds. It hadn't occurred to me that she'd walk, although – thinking about it, now – it should have done. I don't suppose she has much left after the rent and bills are paid. Thanks Lina."

Lina gave him the smile that lit up her face, the smile that lifted the full mouth and raised the high cheekbones to the mass of thick, still-curly hair, now streaked with touches of grey. He reached over and squeezed her hand that was resting round the gin glass, and the touch gave him the same thrill as it had done all those years before when they'd been young and full of life.

"Thanks again. Mile End, you say?"

"I've written down the address. It's off Bow Common Lane. It's a little street called Burley's Close. Strange, really – so many of the names round there are posh sounding and yet the area seems quite run down. I noticed a Portia Crescent and a Waverley Way. In the middle of it, you'll find Tower Hamlets Cemetery Park. You can have a picnic there if you like."

"That sounds nice."

"The man in the café told me. He said that when it was hot people popped in for a sandwich and took it to the cemetery to enjoy a picnic. They do a very nice coffee and a lot of vegetarian alternatives. The owner was born in the East End. Quite a young man – in his late twenties, I should think."

Lina noticed that her husband's eyes had glazed over. She was used to this rather irritating habit, and knew he was picturing where she'd been and where the young woman lived. Bing was walking the streets, pensively.

"You'll need to go now, Bing, if you're going to find her in. She leaves early for work in the morning."

"You don't mind making your own way to Cecilia's?"

"I think I can manage one stop on the Piccadilly Line, Bing. I might even walk," she replied with a laugh.

"I think I'll get the Tube."

"The Central Line will take you all the way to Mile End, but don't fall asleep or you could finish up in Epping."

They made for the Underground station and kissed goodbye at the barrier.

"Thanks again, Lina. Wish me luck."

"Just be careful, Bing. She's a stranger here and she has no reason to trust you."

Almost suffocated by the heat on another Underground journey, Bingham arrived at Mile End station and was met by the rush and tear of traffic on Bow Road. He knew this was the destination of the A11 and wondered how the road that wandered through Norfolk so peacefully could end up in this state.

He turned immediately down Burdett Road only to find it equally busy and was only too pleased to turn off into Bow Common Lane where the traffic moved at a pace more suited to pedestrians. He walked for a while until he passed under the railway viaduct and noticed a small lane signposted with a welcome to Tower Hamlets Cemetery Park. Ahead were the gas works and beyond that, according to his mobile phone, more rush and tear of traffic on St Paul's Way. He wondered what St Paul might have thought had he travelled that road. The whole area seemed surrounded by busy roads and criss-crossed by railway lines; the noise was inescapable.

The residents of Bow Common Lane seemed to possess litter bins and certainly used them, but as he made for Burley's Close Bingham found himself skirting black bags of refuse placed against front doors that opened directly onto the pavement. Some of these had, inevitably, burst open and a one-legged crow was hopping from bag to bag in search of his evening meal.

What a contrast to the area around St James's Park, thought Bingham, and doubted whether the residents of Mile End had benefitted from Britain's place as the third strongest economy in the world.

Burley Close was a dead end occupied by several blocks of old flats. The state of the outside paintwork suggested that they'd been in need of a lick of paint for many years, the wooden window frames were coming apart, beaten by rain and sun, and the concrete surrounds needed a good blast from sand or water to restore their original colour and freshness. Bingham wondered whether the people who had designed them would like to live in Burley Close.

An elderly woman saw him looking at the note Lina had made of the Syrian girl's address and came over to speak, out of a mixture of helpfulness and nosiness. She was a large woman, comfortably fat with a cheery, slab-like face.

"The *Big Issue* girl – that'll be Mariam. That's her flat," she said, smiling and pointing, "She'll probably have finished her dinner by now. She usually gets home about six o'clock."

Bingham, ever fond of the idiosyncrasies of people, smiled at the woman's concern that Mariam should have had time to "finish her dinner". There was a kindliness in the thought that was both ordinary and overwhelming.

"Thank you. Does she live alone?"

"Why?"

The note of suspicion was struck at once. Here was a posh man looking for a young girl and wondering if she was alone.

"I'm looking for a friend of mine – a young man called Robert – and I wondered if he might be at home."

"There's several at home there, dear. Not that the landlord knows and doesn't need to know. One hundred and thirty-eight pound per person per week – do me a favour! Who can afford money like that? People round here work hard – we're not all on benefits despite what the snobs on telly might say – and we need a bit of leeway. Go around to the back and up the stairs. There's only the one door – 4B. You can't miss it."

Bingham followed the woman's advice, easing his way passed the inevitable black bags, hearing pop music or the voices from several television programmes coming from the flats and noticing the smell of carbolic drifting from the open windows. Was it carbolic these days? Bingham wasn't sure: it was a long time since he'd been involved in keeping a house fresh, since Lina commandeered the role.

He knocked and the door was opened immediately by the young woman who recognised him at once and slammed it shut.

"I'm not a policeman," said Bingham, "I've come from Robert's mother, Mabel. She has asked me to find her son."

It was a breathless moment that seemed to run into minutes before the girl opened the door slightly. Bingham could see the chain in place. He stepped back as far as the balcony would allow.

"I'm here to find and help Robert if I can. That's all."

The girl opened the door wider and looked along the balcony and the out over the back courtyards where washing hung on lines above parked cars.

"Come in", she said, and Bingham followed her with a sigh of relief.

The girl looked him up and down, mistrust still fierce in her eyes. Bingham thought that for two pins she'd slit his throat if he turned out to be lying; but beyond the immediate sense of threat there was fear – fear of authority, fear of reprisal.

She had removed her headdress and thick, black hair, lustrously brushed, tumbled to her shoulders; the colour of her hair against the brown of her face was so beautiful that Bingham gazed in amazement. Looking at her, at the bloom on her cheeks, Bingham realised that she was, as he'd supposed, little more than a girl.

"My name is George Bingham," he said, "if you have any doubts, please phone this number."

He fumbled with his mobile phone, trying to locate Mabel Courtney's name, which Lina had inserted for him on the night before he set out. The girl laughed.

"You're just like my grandad," she said. "He can never find anything on his phone."

"You have a grandad here?"

"No – he stayed – but you haven't come about my grandad, have you? Please sit down. May I get you a cup of tea?"

More a conjunction than a clash of cultures, thought Bingham as he smiled his appreciation.

There seemed to be only two rooms to the flat: the living room and the bedroom. He caught a glimpse of what might have been a kitchenette where the girl disappeared to prepare his tea. On the table in the living room, he saw a book open: a modern novel, *The Girl with the Pearl Earring*, that Lina had read but which he'd avoided for no reason other than the fact that everyone said he should read it. Beside the book was a bowl, wiped clean, that must have contained the girl's dinner.

When she returned with the tea – a herbal type that Bingham usually avoided but which tasted fine on his first sip – the girl sat opposite him on a small settee that had seen better days. Her face had relaxed now and contained what Bingham thought was almost an appeal.

"How did you find me?"

"I asked my wife to follow you home today. I'm sorry about that, both on her account and yours, but I needed to ask you about Robert."

"Have you really come to find Robert?"

"Yes."

"Does he know you've come?"

"I don't think so. He hasn't been in touch with his mother since he sent his first note, as far as I know."

"And you're not from the police?"

"No. Do you know where Robert is? You don't have to tell me," he added, hurriedly, as the look of fear returned to haunt her face.

The hesitation was enough for Bingham: she obviously did know or, at least, have some idea, but wasn't prepared to say.

"Who told you about me?"

"Robert has a friend called Alan Vernon. They both work at the Treasury. Alan didn't so much tell me about you as mention that Robert always bought his *Big Issue* from you on a Monday … Monday was the day Robert disappeared. I'm unsure why I approached you, except that I've got nowhere in my search and thought you might be able to help."

Looking the girl over as he spoke, Bingham wondered what the nature of her relationship with Robert

Courtney might be. A shy, retiring young man like him would certainly have been bowled over by such beauty. But the girl herself had a great dignity: there was no chance whatever that they would have been lovers.

"I can be of little help to you."

"I believe your name is Mariam," he said, hoping to appear amiable and ignoring her reservation.

"Who told you that?"

"One of your neighbours: a large lady with a cheery face."

"Vera? Yes, my name is Mariam. We – my family – are Christians. I was named after Mary, the mother of Jesus. My family name is Levy."

Small world thought Bingham. How many people would think of a Syrian girl as being a Christian? Ignorance was widespread and the enemy of world harmony. Sad thoughts for a man who'd spent his life in the service of education.

"I'm pleased to meet you, Mariam, and to know your name. I have two daughters myself – older than you, I think. They are both in their late twenties."

"I'm nineteen."

"I guessed as much," he said, with another smile, "How long have you been here?"

"A year or so."

They'd exchanged names and family details, but Mariam Levy remained unassured.

"I can see that you are protecting Robert," he said, "but he needs to be found. He is in serious trouble and it can only get worse."

"Why?"

"He can't hide forever. He cannot live his life on the run from the police."

"It's not true that he took that money. He wouldn't have done such a thing, and he wouldn't have run."

"But he did run, and that's only made matters worse."

Mariam's eyes caught Bingham's at that moment; it was as though they shared the same thought, and the empathy between them, borne out of a concern for Robert Courtney, grew.

"How many people know that Robert has been here?"

"I didn't say that he had."

"But he has, hasn't he?"

"Yes … Only some of the neighbours and the friends I share the flat with. None of them would say anything."

"Because they distrust authority?"

"Distrust and dislike."

"Had he been here before that Monday?"

"No."

"You were not … friends before then?"

"You mean lovers? No. My family would not approve of such a thing … and neither would I."

"What happened on that Monday morning?"

"Robert always bought his copy of my paper on his way to work. He went in a little late on a Monday so that he would be able to see me on the way, but it isn't far to Westminster on the Piccadilly and Jubilee lines, and so he was never very late."

"Did he tell you that?"

"Yes. He was always eager to explain," said Mariam with a smile.

Bingham thought of the snails and Phil Bassett's comments: 'punctilious' was the word.

"Go on."

"He seemed perfectly happy as he went to work and so I was surprised to see him rushing back before the morning was over."

"Midday?"

"Yes. He was so changed. I've seen fright before but not of that kind. He was in so much hurry that he didn't speak but dashed on by me to where he lives. He came back very soon with a bag under his arm and I stopped him and asked what was wrong. He didn't tell me but said he had to go away for a while. When I asked him where, he said he didn't know. I could tell that he was running away from something or someone and didn't have anywhere to go ..."

Bingham held the pause, refusing to help Mariam out of her moment of indecision.

"I asked him if he needed to hide, and he said yes. In my country we help people like that – people we trust, you understand? You must not draw the wrong conclusion, Mr Bingham ... I gave Robert the key to my flat. It was impulsive I know, but he seemed so frightened and he had always been courteous to me, and you repay respect where I come from. It was my way of saying thank you. Do you understand?"

"Yes, of course. It was an act of kindness. Was he there when you got home at six o'clock?"

"Yes ... He said he'd been accused of stealing some money, a very large sum of money. It had appeared in his bank account, but he didn't know how."

"Did he say why he was running away? Everyone who knows him, including you, has found that to be strange."

"He said he was advised to ... lay low for a while."

Bingham was struck, yet again, by how good was Mariam Levy's English. She'd probably learned the language at home in school and no doubt her current language classes helped, but her grasp of colloquialisms was astonishing. He said so.

"It's a gift," she replied.

"Who gave him that advice?"

"A man called Kevin Pierce. He's Robert's boss. Robert had great respect for him."

Bingham took out the little, leather-bound notebook he carried, and jotted down the name. His memory wasn't what it was ten years ago, and he now had two names of, presumably, eminent civil servants to remember. He thought back to what Dan Jessop had said about the 'Whitehall Loop'; only Bingham didn't see how running away helped Robert Courtney's case.

"Where did Robert stay that night?"

"He stayed here with us. He stayed here for a whole week."

"You and your flat mates realised you might be putting yourselves on the wrong side of the law?"

"Yes, but we didn't mind. In my country a fugitive is given protection from the authorities."

"I take it you went to work as normal, and so Robert was alone during the day?"

"Yes. What difference does that make?"

"Perhaps none. Did he say whether he left the flat at all?"

"We told him not to, and he would have done as we said because we were taking a risk for him."

"Were any of your flatmates here during the day?"

"On and off all the time. We work shifts."

"And your friends were comfortable with Robert being here?"

"I have said so."

Bingham would have liked their names and a chance to talk with each of them. Surely, one of them must have gossiped outside the house. Surely, one of them must know where Robert Courtney was at this moment?

"Do you think your friends would speak with me?"

Mariam Levy smiled. It was all that was needed to put Bingham in his place. The others had almost certainly supported her impulsive action in handing Robert her flat key simply because she was one of them; but they would go no further.

Bingham realised he was in a very strong position, however, and so must the young woman. After all she had told him, Bingham only had to inform the police, and questions would be asked. They might start, quite simply, with illegal occupancy of the flat.

"What impression did you and your friends form of Robert?"

"We all liked him. He is a very sensitive young man. After he had confided his problem, he said little. He would sit, hunched against the wall, staring at the ceiling. When any one of us arrived home that was how we often found him."

"Being confined here for a week, unable to contact the outside world must have driven him mad, mustn't it? I think I would have been keen to get out and attempt to clear my name, to speak to people who I trusted."

"He trusted his boss to clear his name. He supposed Kevin Pierce would contact him."

"How was that to be arranged?"

"Robert was unsure. He said his boss would find a way."

"That would be extremely difficult, wouldn't it, if no one knew where he was?"

Bingham's mind went back to the pile of letters he'd seen, but felt unable to open, on Robert Courtney's desk in the Holborn flat. Had he missed a chance? Was it the expectation that Robert would return to the flat? Was that where the communication would take place?

"When Robert moved on after that first week, was it you who found him another hiding place?"

"Yes, but I am not prepared to say where."

"Is he still there?"

"I don't know. The link in the chain would be broken at every opportunity. Only the last person to move Robert on would know where he is now. I told you I could be of little help."

"But he has been moved on by friends of yours?"

"I don't know. After he left, I know where he went but then we lost track of him."

"What are your feelings towards his plight?"

"What do you mean?"

Bingham felt his usually equable nature being tested by the deliberate obtuseness of an intelligent girl; had he been an ill-tempered man, he would have lost it at that moment.

"Robert needs to be found. If you liked him, it would be a good idea for you to assist in the search. I take it that you don't want him to be on the run for the rest of his life."

It wasn't a question, and the young woman knew it. There was no smile on her face or his when Bingham rose from the chair, bid her goodbye and left the flat.

Chapter Five
THE JOURNALIST

Bingham became aware of the man soon after they passed Bethnal Green station. He knew he'd seen the face before but couldn't place where. It wasn't until the train had emptied at Liverpool Street and the man still sat in the same place, glancing at Bingham occasionally while keeping his head down behind a newspaper whenever Bingham sought to hold his gaze, that Bingham remembered seeing him at the flats after he'd walked out on Mariam Levy.

Vera had been waiting for him, this time purely out of nosiness. Bingham thanked her for the assistance she'd given and said that "Miss Levy had been most helpful" when the man appeared from somewhere behind the block of dilapidated housing.

He hadn't really taken much notice of him at the time. Why should he? The man was simply another resident. And there was no reason to take any account of him now. After all, he had every right to be travelling on the same train as Bingham. Except that he made Bingham uneasy.

It wasn't just the cloak of obfuscation surrounding Robert Courtney that troubled Bingham regarding the stranger: a cloak stitched together mainly by those who claimed to be his friends or, at the very least, like him. It was more that the man struck Bingham as being 'odd'. It was an easy enough description – out of date, perhaps, but less complicated to understand than whatever the modern pop-psychological equivalent might be.

He was of the type generally described as 'ferret-faced'. He was small, scrawny and hunched; his shoulders were up round his ears as though he was keeping the rain from running down his neck. His face was pasty, with the unhealthy look of a man who lived on takeaways. The eyes were small, brown and shifty.

Bingham saw him as a loner: one who sat in his bedroom, or wherever he might inhabit, brooding, dwelling on unsolved mysteries while life passed him by, avoiding the mystery of life itself while pretending to be the possessor of secret knowledge. Secrets, Bingham decided, were this man's bread and butter; he'd rather possess knowledge he thought exclusive to himself than cook his own dinner. Such men, Bingham thought, would be better off popping down the local for a pint than sitting in their rooms pretending they were somebody special.

At Holborn, Bingham left the train and wandered out into the street where he'd spoken with Mariam Levy the previous morning. The night was still uncomfortably hot, and people were in shirt sleeves: jackets over their arms, collars soaked in sweat. Bingham looked around and asked himself what he was doing in Holborn when Cecilia lived in Bloomsbury. It was only then he realized he'd meant to continue on the Piccadilly Line to Russell Square, from there he knew the way to his daughter's. Perhaps it wasn't far to walk. He'd ask.

Standing like a lost soul on the pavement, Bingham suddenly remembered a pub he and Lina had called in on their way from a show at the Apollo Theatre during the summer. The Princess Louise was its name: a genuine Victorian pub with wooden floors and panelling, booths and snugs where one could sit quietly, a long wooden bar and a narrow passageway as you entered from the road. He remembered enjoying an oatmeal stout and Lina being pleased that all the beers were either vegetarian or vegan.

The memory was enough and soon Bingham was installed on a comfortable settee in the main body of the pub enjoying an Old Brewery Bitter. It was now after ten o'clock, and it had been a long day for both him and Lina. Hopefully, she'd be settled down with her daughter and, possibly, grandson, if Bruno had not gone to bed.

Not for the first time, Bingham wondered what he was doing drifting about the country's capital looking for a young man who didn't want to be found. He'd need to speak with Mariam Levy and Alan Vernon again. He knew that to be the case, but also knew he had no authority to do so. He trusted that his sudden exit and her knowledge that he could, if he wished, make matters difficult for her and her flatmates would be enough to ginger her up without him pressing the point, which he knew he would have the decency not to do.

It was while these thoughts passed across his mind that he noticed the ferret-faced man standing at the bar, watching Bingham's reflection in the mirror. Even for Bingham, a man much averse to gossip and jumping to conclusions, becoming conscious of the same man in his presence in three different places within an hour of each appearance was too much, and he strolled over to the bar.

"You seem to have something to say to me. Perhaps I can buy you a drink and we can have a chat."

The man's tongue flicked across his bottom lip in a gesture typical in Bingham's experience of someone caught in the act of doing something they shouldn't.

"What do you mean?" asked the stranger, in an inane attempt at bluff, reminding Bingham of the many schoolboys who came up with the similar "What me, sir!"

"I saw you in Burley's Close, you were watching me on the Tube and now we meet in a listed building. Let's have a chat. Better out than in."

The man laughed, perhaps at Bingham's slight vulgarity, perhaps because he was unsettled by Bingham's apparent knowledge concerning the Princess Louise.

"I'll have whisky. I don't drink beer at this time of night. It unsettles my stomach."

Bingham ordered himself another bitter, a whisky for his new-found friend and they settled themselves in a cosy corner with Bingham's back to the wall so that he could hear what the man had to say.

For a while they sat in silence, Bingham being in no hurry and the stranger not knowing where to begin. Bingham took the chance to look the man over. He was shabbily dressed, and Bingham guessed he had little money to waste on new clothes. There was also an odour about the man, not unpleasant but simply stale as though he sat for most of his time in one place: a man of enclosed spaces rather than the open air.

"My name's George Bingham," he said, at last, to move the conversation forward.

Again, the tongue flicked across the man's lower lip and his mouth tightened indicating a reluctance to divulge such a secret to Bingham or anyone else; but Bingham's smile held his eyes and eventually he said:

"Stan."

"Stan …?"

"Stan Chalfont."

"Please to meet you, Stan. I take it you know what I was doing in Burley Close?"

"I know all about it."

"That puts you ahead of me in the game."

A smile crossed Stan's narrow eyes, and Bingham knew they were on their way.

"I know all about them … them in the flat. Four of them in one flat – I could tell."

"But you won't. It's your secret."

"Dead right."

"I suppose you know what I was enquiring about, too?"

"I don't miss much. I have information they want. If they knew what I knew."

"About the missing young man?"

"I saw him come."

"What time was that?" asked Bingham, wishing to verify at least this fact before being led on some wild goose chase.

"It was half past one."

"You seem very sure of the time."

"I don't make mistakes with time. I always have my lunch at one o'clock and it takes me half-an-hour to eat it. I chew everything."

"What day was it?"

"Monday."

"How can you be sure about that?"

"I had toasted cheese for lunch. I always have toasted cheese on a Monday."

At least there's going to be an element of truth in what this man has to say, thought Bingham: so far, so good.

"He arrived with a holdall. Did he seem to know where he was going?"

"He looked around a bit. The numbering of the flats makes no sense. Then she came out."

"She?"

"Vera! She has her nose into everything. She showed him to the door. Curious she was, but I knew."

Stan paused and looked round the bar, but no one was listening. Everyone else was involved in their own conversations.

"I read the papers. I don't miss anything. I have to keep my eyes and ears open. I need to know what's going on."

"What paper do you read?"

"I go to the library. I read them all, every morning from nine o'clock to twelve o'clock. It didn't make the television, did it, so she wouldn't know, but I know."

"You recognised the young man?" asked Bingham, who had known nothing of Robert's disappearance until Lina told him and couldn't recall having seen Robert's photograph in any newspaper.

"I didn't have to: I can put two and two together. He was nervous, on the run. I knew it was him."

"But not on that morning," said Bingham. "It hadn't yet been in the papers."

"Afterwards, thinking about it. Seeing him arrive like that and then reading it in the papers. It had to make sense. It had to be him."

"How was he dressed?"

"Jeans and a leather jacket. What's that got to do with it?"

"He wasn't wearing his work clothes," replied Bingham. "He'd taken time to change. I'm glad you noticed, Stan. You're very observant. During the time he was at the flat, did he ever go out during the day?"

"Never! He never moved in daylight, nor after dark."

"You wouldn't have seen him in the mornings, would you – not if you were at the library?"

"I didn't go that week. I got a paper in and watched. He never moved."

"You watched all day and night?"

"I wasn't going to miss anything."

"You'd have made a good policeman."

"Too short, too thin – they didn't want me, but I could tell them things now. You're a private eye, aren't you?"

The last thing Bingham wanted was to be thought of in that way, but he could see Stan's weakness and went along with the deception.

"Yes," he replied, "I'm looking for Robert Courtney."

"I can tell you where he is."

Bingham's heart leapt, but cautiously. He wasn't to be taken in by the likes of Stan, but perhaps there was a slight hope that the man who knew everything might point him in some direction.

"I saw them take him away."

"Them?"

"The likes of her: foreigners. They came for him in a van."

"Go on."

A look of utter joy blended with a deep craftiness spread across Stan's face. This was his moment; this was where he possessed the knowledge that eluded both Bingham and the authorities.

"I heard them. I'd just been to the toilet and heard them: the sound of the van and their voices whispering."

"What time was this?"

"What time do you think! It was one o'clock in the morning, when the rest of us were supposed to be in bed, but I was watching."

"Was Vera about?" asked Bingham, eager that she might corroborate Stan's story.

"Not her. She goes to bed at half past ten every night, just after the news. I hear her check her doors and flush the toilet. She makes a cup of tea, and all the lights go off in her flat."

"How do you know she makes a cup of tea?" asked Bingham, unable to help himself.

"The kettle – you can hear it boil – and the clink of the cup on the saucer."

"What did you do when you heard the footsteps and the voices?"

"I can see the yard from my window. The van pulled up and one of them opened the doors. Then she came down with him they're after. They bundled him into the back."

"How many of them were there?"

"Her and the two men – foreigners like herself. They bundled him in and shut the doors quickly. I heard them whispering among themselves, and then they drove off and she came back up."

"Was the yard lit?"

"What do you mean?"

"I was wondering if you were able to see the number plate of the van."

Utter joy again passed over the small man's face. As if he was as stupid as the rest!

"Did you think I'd forget to take the number?"

"I hoped you might have done. If you have, it can be traced."

"No need for that."

He still held the high ground against Bingham's undoubted ignorance, and waited, exultantly, for the next question.

"Why?"

"Because I know where they took him."

Bingham held his excitement in check, not simply because Stan seemed to offer a lead but because what he'd said might complicate rather than clarify the affair. Had Marian Levy acted purely out of kindness or was she involved rather more deeply with Robert Courtney that he'd at first believed? Had the boy from Northfield become entangled with these people? A young man in a big city was vulnerable in so many ways.

"You traced the van yourself?"

"I didn't have to."

"Go on."

"Think it out for yourself, Mr Bingham. Why wouldn't I need to trace the van?"

"Because you knew the men?"

"No."

"I'm lost."

"It was a van, Mr Bingham," explained Stan, as though he was enlightening his teacher, "What can you tell me about vans?"

"They're used for business and have the name of the firm on the side?"

Stan's face fell as his moment of absolute power faded.

"Smart Image Dry Cleaning," he said, "in capitals on the side."

"Knowing you, Stan, you took the phone number as well, didn't you?" said Bingham to regain his informer's confidence.

"The number and the website." replied Stan, his self-esteem partly restored.

Bingham was exhausted. For the second or maybe third time that evening he told himself what a long day it had been, and he still faced a walk of indeterminate length. He needed another drink before the bar closed and couldn't risk a beer in case he found no toilet on his walk.

"Do you fancy another whisky?" he asked Stan.

Having ordered the two, he returned to their settee and sighed.

"I'm very grateful for all your help, Stan," he said. "What can I do for you in return?"

"I don't want money," was the snappish reply.

"I didn't suppose you did."

"I want to know what's going on. I want to be there when you catch him."

Bingham wasn't inclined to make any such promise and was relieved when the barmaid called 'Time, gentlemen, please'. He returned the drinks glasses to the bar and asked the barmaid if he could walk from where he was to Russell Square, since he didn't feel inclined to ask Stan. She laughed, and Bingham, not for the first time that day, felt like a little boy lost in the big city.

"Do you know the area at all, sir?"

"I know Red Lion Street."

"Good – well go there and then on to Red Lion Square. From the Square turn left into Proctor Street and immediate right into Catton Street. Then all you do is follow Southampton Row. It'll take you straight to Russell Square. It's not far – less than a mile, I should think you'll be in bed in half-an-hour."

Fifteen minutes later Bingham said goodbye to Stan on the pavement outside the pub. Bingham watched him disappear with the crowd making for the underground station and turned his face towards his daughter's home.

Unusually, he was late up the following morning, "his fourth day in the Great Wen", he told himself when Lina brought him a cup of black coffee and a warm croissant at half past ten. Bingham glanced at his watch, realizing he was too late to catch Mariam Levy before she left for work, having hoped he might persuade her to close at least one link in the chain.

"I thought you might like me to wake you. It's coffee, and I know how much you hate being late up."

"Thanks, Lina," he replied, kissing her gently on the soft lips he'd come to love so much.

"Besides, Dan Jessop – isn't he a charming man? – has arranged for you to meet a journalist friend of his for lunch."

"I don't like journalists, Lina. You know that. He's just sniffing round for a story."

"Nevertheless, we'll meet him and find out what he's got to say."

"We – are you coming?"

"Well, don't you want me to? I can always find something else to do."

"That's not what I meant, and you know it. I just didn't think you'd be interested – or might have something better to do."

In truth, he was pleased Lina was coming. He had no desire to converse with any journalist and knew he could rely on Lina to do most of the talking, while he listened for any gems that might fall. The good listener is a vital component of any conversation.

"You'll like the venue," was Lina's reply.

The venue was a city pub Bingham had been meaning to visit for several years. Ye Olde Cheshire Cheese in Fleet Street was reputedly used by Dickens as the place where Sydney Carton took Charles Darnay in *A Tale of Two Cities*, a book Bingham admired.

He and Lina made their way down a narrow alley and entered a world of wood panelling, gloomy lighting, bricks underfoot and an interminable number of floors that opened onto numerous bars.

Their host, Lionel Bliss, was waiting for them, less famous but no less welcoming than the pub's interior. He waved them into the Cheshire Bar, where plaques on the wall showed photographs of famous people who had once frequented the establishment. The Cheshire Bar also provided discreet seating in the form of settles where the journalist could talk without being overheard and where Bingham would stand a chance of hearing him.

Lionel Bliss, having ordered his guests' food and settled them over a drink (an Old Brewery Bitter for Bingham, an organic lager for Lina and a craft beer for himself) wasted no time in getting to the point.

"Dan tells me that you're trying to track down young Courtney, and – I'll make no bones about it – I'm looking for a good story."

"Before you say any more, Mr Bliss, may I ask if you have anything new to tell us?"

Lina – used as she was to Bingham's direct manner, which she considered bordered on rudeness at times – threw him a glance of muted disapproval.

"Lionel – please. Yes and no. I have nothing directly to tell you about young Courtney, but I know about a similar *case* that might give you an insight into what could have happened."

"Please go on, Lionel," said Lina, throwing Bingham another glance warning him to remain quiet.

"Some time ago, during the Kosovo conflict, an attack was authorised on what was thought to be an enemy stronghold. This resulted in many civilian casualties. Since the NATO bombing campaign lacked the backing of the UN Security Council there was considerable concern in Whitehall that the death of civilians, which included women and children, might result in a media backlash against the government's decision to involve our country, and so a series of half-truths was fed to the media."

"Why didn't the government simply acknowledge that a terrible misjudgement had occurred?" asked Lina. "The public broadly approved our part in providing air support."

"You might wonder, mightn't you, Lina? But they didn't and, of course, journalists and one or two troublesome MPs immediately suspected a smoke screen. They started to ferret around, turning up increasingly awkward questions that led to more dissembling. After the war, questions continued to be asked and so the original half-truths became a full-blown cover-up."

"Not to do so would have involved admitting the original half-truths," said Lina.

"You've hit the proverbial nail on the head, Lina."

Lina looked at Bingham who was gazing across the room at nothing.

"I don't see how this ties in with Robert Courtney's disappearance," she said.

"I'm coming to that. The problem with any cover-up is that everyone involved must tell the same story. When an investigation was considered unavoidable, certain discrepancies in the stories of different people emerged."

"As people like you asked for more and more details the web of deceit became even more tangled," suggested Lina.

"Quite! You might say the hole they were digging became ever deeper."

"The credibility gap widened," suggested Lina, partly to annoy Bingham, who she could see was irritated by the metaphors.

"The potential for embarrassment was growing and something had to be done. A young civil servant – young but not inexperienced – was given the task of producing what one might call the 'authorized version' of events; one that would satisfy the media and close the matter down. He presented his paper at a top-level meeting, and it was rejected as being too 'open'. He was asked to 'adjust' some of the details: 'spread a little fog around' was one expression used.

He was unhappy about this further subterfuge because he felt his original paper had clarified the matter without pointing the blame at any particular individual. He also knew that to adjust his report would involve him in the original half-truths. He went to his senior officer to lodge his concern. He was relieved from duty and never seen again."

"How do you know all this?"

"Before he disappeared, he wrote a letter, enclosing his original report, to a journalist friend."

"You?"

"No – a senior colleague of mine."

Lina gazed, silently, at Lionel Bliss as though he was part of the subterfuge. Bingham watched his wife without speaking. He could see she was wondering how the young civil servant concerned had been silenced.

"You don't mean that he was killed?"

"I don't know. He might simply have retreated from public life with a large pay-off."

"But felt guilty about it and so sent his report to your friend?"

"Something of the sort."

"But Robert Courtney had only been in the department five years. He wouldn't have been entrusted with anything similar, would he?"

"He was a very bright young man, and way ahead of the game in matters economic."

"I don't believe it," said Lina, emphatically, "Bing and I knew Robert when he was a child. We know Mabel Courtney. There are certain people who are quite incapable of doing anything dishonourable and Robert is one of them."

The journalist smiled a worldly smile that irritated Lina, who disliked the cynical knowingness of journalists as much as her husband did. She glanced at

Bingham, who refused to meet her eyes and was apparently absorbed in what was happening in the passage as tourists wandered in, wondering at the maze of rooms and where they might find a seat.

Lina, not normally at a loss for something to say, wasn't sure how to pursue the conversation in Robert Courtney's interests and was relieved when their food arrived; she and Lionel Bliss enjoyed fish and chips, served with mushy peas on pseudo-newspaper in a wooden tray, while Bingham forked a vegetarian risotto silently from his plate. He nodded to the young barman, who had been most courteous, and indicated their drinks. It was only when they'd been replenished, and he'd finished his risotto and was helping Lina out with her chips that Bingham spoke.

"You'll be able to obtain a copy of this report, I take it?"

"Why?" asked Lionel Bliss.

"Will you?"

"I don't see why not."

"Thank you. If you'll drop it off at my daughter's address – I'm sure she won't mind as long as you don't make a nuisance of yourself – I'd be grateful."

"I don't see what you're driving at, Mr Bingham."

"Nor do I."

"You've nothing to give me?"

"No."

"Do you believe he's innocent?"

"I don't know."

"If he is, then someone else has questions to answer."

"It would seem so."

"This is my number, Mr Bingham. If you come across anything that would throw any light into the darkness of this case, I'd appreciate it if you gave me a ring."

He handed Bingham a card bearing his photograph and the name of several newspapers, which Bingham tucked into his wallet and rose to leave.

"Mr Bliss."

"Yes."

"There's nothing for you to print except speculation and that would harm this young man. Your story will arrive in time."

"Then you do believe he's innocent."

Bingham rose to shake the journalist's hand, eager that he should not resume his seat, and heaved a sigh of relief to Lina when they were alone.

"Are you any further forward, Bing?"

"I'm asking myself what Robert Courtney's state of mind is at this moment. On the one hand he knows his career is in ruins, his family name is dishonoured, he is being hidden by people he doesn't know, he is being ignored by someone he thought was a friend, the police are seeking to arrest him and his mother is distraught."

"And on the other hand?"

"You tell me."

"He's turned his back on his career, with a quarter of a million in the bank isn't overly bothered about his family name or his mother, is nicely placed with his new friends, has turned his back on old colleagues and just needs to keep one step ahead of the police until he can safely leave the country?"

"Lina, you can always tell a false note from one hit squarely. Do you fancy meeting the lady you followed the other day? She's the only lever I have now, apart from Alan Vernon, who isn't answering my calls. Now, before I ask if you'd like to undertake another shadowing job, perhaps you'd look at that app of yours and find out how we get from Fleet Street to Holborn?"

Chapter Six
THE UNDER SECRETARY

Bingham waited anxiously by his daughter's window, waiting for Lina to return and promising himself that he would not involve her any further in the disappearance of Robert Courtney, a name with which he was becoming increasingly irritated.

The unseasonably hot weather had to break sometime. For days, Bingham had been hoping for a storm to relieve the unwelcome humidity that caused his clothes to cling to him like propolis to a hive, but he didn't want it to break just yet, not before Lina had returned home.

He knew he'd been anxious all evening, hiding it in the way expected of him as a child, eager not to worry his grandson or his daughter who were now watching television in the sitting room, cuddled together on the sofa.

It was getting dark. Always at about this time in September the nights seemed to draw in suddenly. The streetlamps were not yet lit and it was still possible to discern the black clouds as they gathered overhead, but soon all would be immersed in darkness. At the far end of the street, the pillar box was still visibly red, and he could just about discern the passers-by, coats open, umbrellas in hand.

He and Lina had waylaid Mariam Levy, marched her into the nearest coffee bar and laid down the law. Only she could instigate the first step in linking the chain that would, hopefully, lead to Robert Courtney, unless she wanted Bingham to approach Smart Image Dry Cleaning or, if not Bingham, the police. Someone had to find the young man. Wasn't it preferable that should be a friend?

Alone with Bingham, the young Syrian might have refused, but Lina exerted a quietly persuasive influence, assuring her that Bingham was "concerned for Robert", fearing he might be "becoming increasingly desperate".

"What made you say I thought Robert might become desperate?" he asked as they left the girl and made their way to St James's Park.

"Bing, I haven't been married to you for over thirty years without knowing what you're feeling."

"Umm," was all he said in reply.

The Piccadilly, Northern and District lines took them to St James's Park underground station, a subterranean journey that had them sweltering in the heat and gasping for some fresh air, but which settled them on a seat overlooking the Treasury. Bingham explained that he wanted to "put pressure on Alan Vernon".

"He knows something, Lina. Robert wrote to him and he has refused to show me the letter. If you'd be kind enough to follow him home, I'll pay him a visit this evening."

She was now later back than Bingham had expected. Given that Alan Vernon lived no more than an hour away from his place of work and that Lina had begun following him when he left at five o'clock, she should have been home soon after seven; it was now eight o'clock and there was no sign of her.

All along, Bingham had sensed not so much danger as a threat in the Robert Courtney business: a threat to happiness, a threat to life. He didn't like the idea of his wife being under any kind of threat and his concern had become irritability.

"She'll be all right, Dad," said Cecilia, coming into the room and placing her hand on his shoulder, "She probably knows London better than you do."

Bingham was glad he'd had daughters; sons were fine, but you couldn't put your arms round them and be comforted in quite the same way. He smiled to himself, puzzled by his daughter's idea that he was concerned about his wife being lost in London. His disquiet wasn't so specific; it was a feeling of unease.

He was to remain in that state for another half-an-hour at which time Lina walked into Cecilia's flat, just as the heavens opened, with a tale to tell.

She had followed Alan Vernon with no trouble at all. The young man had taken the Victoria Line and alighted at the Islington and Highbury Underground Station. All that oppressed either of them was the heat of that day; otherwise, his journey to and from work could not have been less stress free.

Once they'd moved away from the busy area around the station, Lina found herself in a quiet residential road with open parkland to her left and freshly painted houses to her right, each with their basements shielded from the pavement by low, black railings. Young women walked their toddlers or propelled them in push chairs along wide pavements, while older children kicked balls on the grass. Seats, where people sat and chatted, were placed at regular intervals. There was no sign of litter. Cared-for was the phrase that came to Lina.

Turning into a side road, she passed neat, privet hedges and eventually came to what she thought might be a crescent where the house fronts were more open. Alan Vernon stopped before a converted coach house, took a key from his pocket and approached a door that stood alongside the large doors of what was now a garage.

"I couldn't see the point of coming back to tell you where he lived, Bing," she said, as they sat at Cecilia's table enjoying a glass of wine with the meal Cecilia had re-heated for her mother. "It would only have meant you turning out later in the evening, and so I thought I'd talk to the young man myself."

Alan Vernon had seemed startled when she spoke to him and attempted to enter the house before she could engage him in conversation, but Lina was nimble. She reached the door and raised an admonitory hand, causing Alan to pause in the doorway.

"I knew he wouldn't slam the door in a woman's face. I could have been his mother. I told him who I was and that I only wanted to have a quick word, and he let me in."

Alan Vernon showed Lina into what he called his reception room. It was spotless. The wooden floor was buffed to a high polish putting at risk anyone who might step onto either of the two rugs; a series of deep, open shelves arranged in squares adorned part of one wall and these contained books, discs, a collection of pristine LPs and one or two ornaments, including two vases sporting flowers; on a low unit was Alan's turntable and compact disc player; a small table was placed in one corner of the room, which also served as a dining area. Lina was offered a cup of tea, which Alan Vernon served in a china tea set like the one she remembered her mother using.

"I like vintage things," he said, "but only in a modern setting. I wouldn't want to live in an old building with all its memories."

"This coach house must be date back a century or so," replied Lina.

"Oh yes, but you wouldn't know it, would you? It was completely re-furbished some years ago. It's a listed building … I can see you're puzzled … wondering how a young civil servant can afford such a place? My father bought it when the area was less *sought after*, as they say. It proved to be a sound investment. I suppose he'll want to sell it one day, when he retires, if he retires, but now it's very handy for me and he's only too pleased for me to use it."

Despite his reservations at letting Lina into his home, Alan Vernon now appeared relaxed, and it was obvious he enjoyed talking. Lina encouraged him, having noticed during her time as a professional opera singer that gay young men usually enjoyed talking to women.

He talked her through the neighbourhood and through his years at university, explaining that his love of classical music and of the theatre, particularly the musical theatre since he found "serious plays singularly unattractive", stemmed from his own mother's love of music. He paused occasionally to indicate a particular recording he admired and trotted off the names of opera singers long since dead.

When Lina shared with him some aspects of her own career, particularly her love of Puccini's operas, he listened without interrupting, quite rapt in the conversation.

"It was when I was singing with the English National Opera that I met Bing," she said, after half-an-hour or so. "The ENO were performing *The Turn of the Screw*, and Bing came along. He's very fond of Britten."

"I can't say the same," replied Alan Vernon, "He's too austere for me, but I can imagine George liking his work. He seemed a very sensitive man, almost shy."

No one had ever described her husband as 'shy' before, but there was some truth in the observation, and Lina said so.

"You can trust him, Alan. He only wants to help your friend Robert."

"I know, and I'm ashamed. It was rude not to answer his phone calls."

"Why didn't you?"

"I was frightened."

"Of what Robert had to say in the letter?"

"Yes."

"Did it implicate someone at the Treasury?"

"Yes."

"Sir Kevin Pierce?"

"How did you know about him?"

"Bing is very persistent," said Lina, with what she hoped was a reassuring laugh.

"He isn't a 'sir'," said Alan, "He's only an OBE."

"Why are you frightened of him – him only being an OBE?"

Alan Vernon laughed, appreciating the humour and the fact Lina shared his spite.

"I'm not frightened of Kevin Pierce. It's what Robert had to say in his letter that worried me."

Lina waited, not wanting to push the young man into revealing secrets but desperate that he should. Alan Vernon pursed his lips and shrugged his shoulders, turning his head slightly to one side and closing his eyes. When he opened them, his eyebrows lifted and he gazed across the reception room, looking out of the high, narrow window at the black sky.

It was obvious to Lina that here was a young man who enjoyed a gossip, who trusted her and wanted to share what he knew, but without complications.

"You see," he said, eventually turning to face her across the little dining table, "it's a question of not letting the side down."

"Will what you read in the letter help Bing to find Robert?"

"I'm not sure that would be in his best interests."

"But he must want to prove his innocence?"

"Yes, of course he does."

"He cannot remain on the run forever."

Alan Vernon looked Lina straight in the eyes as she made this remark and was clearly about to make a comment of his own but decided against it.

"Please, Alan, let Bing pursue this on your friend's behalf. If anything, Robert said in that letter can help my husband do that, let me know what it was."

"You're asking me to betray my friend or my department."

"In that case, I hope you have the courage to betray your department," replied Lina.

At first, the young man looked shocked and then proud, as though in his imagination he was about to face the guns of the enemy.

"Forster once said that if he ever had to choose between betraying his friends or his country, he'd choose to betray his country," he said.

Lina waited, patiently.

"Robert came across a report. I don't know what it contained because Robert wouldn't tell me. It was called *Whoop/s*, with a forward slash between the 'p' and the 's'. Don't look puzzled, Lina. All civil service departments have a rather black sense of humour. It helps us survive under adverse circumstances such as when the public wants to know something, we'd rather they didn't. You'll notice where the forward slash is placed in the name of the report. 'Whoop' is a cry of joy whereas 'whoops' is an error, a mistake for which someone is responsible. It's clear that the report was a financial one of considerable importance and that if its contents were leaked then someone very, very eminent was in dire trouble."

"You thought trouble would follow once the report was known publicly?"

"Yes."

"Did Robert have a hand in writing it?"

"I don't think so, but I think he came across it while working on something else."

"Do you think it will increase his danger once this news gets out?"

"I don't know. I don't know how far it poses a threat to the service. The reason I was reluctant to share what Robert had said was because I thought it would be traced back to me."

"And jeopardise your career chances?"

"Yes. I've never been particularly brave and, apart from that, I didn't want to disappoint my parents."

Bingham and his wife had worked their way through a whole bottle of the wine before Lina completed her story.

"He was in tears when I left him, Bing. He knew he'd let his friend down – a friend who had stood by him."

"I can imagine," replied Bingham, "Thanks, Lina. This doesn't lead us to Robert – at least not directly – but it should open the door to Kevin Pierce OBE."

Bingham lay awake all night; try as he might, he could not find sleep. At home, he would simply have slid out of bed and gone to his study where he might curl up on the couch, annoying the dogs but leaving Lina in peace. In his daughter's flat, he could only refrain from tossing and turning by staring into the darkness of the ceiling.

He tried the old trick whereby he closed his eyes and pictured a mass of whirling, white shapes; they might have been snow or stars, but they always ended up contracting to one dark point and disappearing into the void beyond, taking Bingham with them. But that night, each time they vanished, Bingham woke with a jerk rather than fell into blessed sleep.

Sometime before the light of dawn brought relief, he thought he heard the milkman and the paper boy, but these were only the sounds of his imagination returning to childhood because Cecilia's double glazing removed any chance that he might become aware of the next day naturally.

When Lina woke him with a cup of tea, he realized he must have dozed off eventually, but it was an uneasy dozing in some place where his mind remained active, so that he felt ragged rather than refreshed; ragged but relieved because somewhere in the darkness his mind had cleared.

He'd never been one to prepare for interviews in too much detail, preferring to let the conversation take its natural course and seize the moment; but this one would be different. He must seem to be the possessor of the knowledge he was corroborating; he needed to set an experienced official, a man used to artifice and stratagems, back on his heels.

What seemed to be the same steady trickle of people made its way in and out of the Treasury building, pursuing the same ends (fresh air, government business or a smoke) and dressed in the same casual manner; and he was welcomed by the same doorman with his high-visibility body warmer who graced Bingham's second visitor pass (courtesy of Dan Jessop again) with the same smile.

The young woman at the reception desk – who he greeted, courtesy of Alan Vernon, as Inaya – did not, on this occasion, steer him into the park, but replaced the surprise at his knowing her name with a frown when Bingham mentioned Kevin Pierce by name and insisted he had an appointment. She made a phone call that brought a young man, this time in the smart striped suit Bingham expected, from the depths of the building after Bingham had waited for about twenty minutes, having refused to move or even sit.

"There's no record of you having an appointment with Mr Pierce this morning, Mr ... eh ... Bingham," he said.

"That's because I don't," replied Bingham, nettled by the deliberate pauses, "It was merely a strategy to get you, or someone like you, out here. Do I assume you are Mr Pierce's clerk?"

"I'm his Executive Officer."

"Good. Tell your boss that I must see him concerning the whereabouts of Robert Courtney and his report. I have all day and am prepared to wait until the sun goes down or longer, if necessary. Stress that I have mentioned his name only in your hearing. Is that clear?"

Bingham wasn't sure whether the expression with which he was favoured was one of anger or mere irritation, but he was pleased to have made an impression.

"If you would care to wait …," was all the young man said, leaving Bingham to interpret the pause for himself, as he turned back through the door from where he had come.

Bingham followed before the door clicked-to and before anyone might think of calling for the security men. The young man looked him up and down, decided against making a fuss and led Bingham down numerous corridors, smartly painted in cream and gold, to a beautiful wooden door that someone who knew the art had french-polished superbly.

"If you would care to wait …," repeated the young man (indicating by his manner and the look he delivered down a long, rather aristocratic, nose that he didn't really give a toss whether Bingham cared or not) who then tapped on the door and entered, shutting it smartly against Bingham.

It was a long wait, but Bingham had expected such a strategy: keeping someone waiting softens them up and dulls the brain. He didn't doubt, however, that he'd been kept under strict surveillance: not ten minutes passed without someone coming along the corridor and ignoring him.

He'd arrived just after coffee time, and the lunch hour came and went. Bingham sat patiently, a characteristic Lina said endeared him to the dogs.

When the polished door eventually opened, the same young man waved him into the presence of Mr Kevin Pierce. Bingham was amused to think of the man as 'Mr' because his whole appearance, and no doubt his expectation, suggested that 'Sir' was only waiting around the corner.

He was a tall man and looked distinguished in every way from the handmade shoes to the crown of thick, wavy, white hair; even his suit, half-way through the working day, was without creases, and the smooth tie, though knotted neatly in a Windsor, looked untouched by hand. He gazed at Bingham for a short while, allowing his guest to admire his magnificence and then extended his hand.

"I am given to believe that you are searching for Robert Courtney, Mr Bingham. Am I to assume that you are what the American movies call a private investigator?"

The heavy attempt at humour marked the man as out of touch even to someone as old-fashioned in his tastes as Bingham, who wasn't sure whether the Under Secretary was trying to make himself sound approachable or merely out to amuse his Executive Officer.

"His mother asked me to find him."

"You are a friend of Mrs Courtney?"

"We live in the same village – Northfield, just to the north of Ipswich. I believe you have yet to meet Mabel Courtney."

If the Under Secretary flinched it wasn't noticeable. He smiled affably and pursued the pleasantries.

"It's a charming part of East Anglia. Quite close to Constable Country."

The Under Secretary addressed his last remark to his Executive Officer and then turned to Bingham.

"I understand you have news of Robert, Mr Bingham?"

"Moves are afoot that I hope will lead us to finding him, Mr Pierce."

"How can I help you?"

"Once we find Robert, I believe it will take a great deal of persuasion to lure him from his hiding place. It would, therefore, be helpful to know why he considered it necessary to hide in the first place."

"You are familiar with what occurred?"

"I'm familiar with several versions of what occurred. I was hoping you might be able to verify the truth. Do you mind if I sit down? Waiting in the corridor for so long has quite stiffened the sinews," replied Bingham with a smile.

Genuine embarrassment clouded the handsome face. A frosty glare was thrown at the Executive Officer who promptly moved a chair into place on the door side of the Under Secretary's large desk. The man himself retreated to the far side and for the first time Bingham, freed from being cornered by the two men, was able to look about him.

The room was wood panelled and veneered bookcases lined the walls, but the room was dominated by the desk, which was of the Victorian mahogany pedestal type. Bingham knew something about wood from his solicitor father's hobby and learned even more from his daughter, Cecilia, whenever she craved his company on her search of antique shops.

Bingham was struck by the difference between this inner sanctum of the Treasury and its outward appearance; it was almost as though the reception area and the casual dressers who spilled onto the pavement were a front for something much older and much more knowing.

Once seated, Mr Pierce waited with a smile until Bingham continued.

"What kind of employee was Robert?"

"He was a very pleasant young man and extremely able. We had high hopes that he would be fast-tracked through the Treasury to a directorial position – but I'm sure you are already acquainted with his dedication and expertise, Mr Bingham."

"He came to you five years ago highly recommended from one of the most prestigious of Oxford colleges, didn't he?"

"We only take on the best at Robert's level, Mr Bingham."

"What was your impression of him as a person?"

"Our officers' private lives are … private."

"I meant as a person when he was at work. How did he approach his work?"

"Did you know him?"

"He was at school with my younger son," replied Bingham, evasively.

"Then you may already realise that Robert was very intense. The word 'mistake' wasn't in his dictionary, so to speak."

"But he worked creatively, and got on well with his colleagues?"

"Very much so."

"There was no one who would claim they either disliked or distrusted him?"

"Certainly, that is so."

"So, what he is alleged to have done must have come as a complete surprise?"

"Put in that way, I must agree with you."

"I have been given to understand by several people – people quite unconnected with each other – that it was you who advised Robert Courtney to 'lay low for a while'. Why was that?"

Bingham's abruptness had occasionally cut through many a shield of lies or evasiveness, but the Under Secretary was made of sterner stuff.

"People who, I imagine, received this information from Robert himself?"

"Mainly – yes."

"Completely, Mr Bingham. If it were true, only Robert would have had such knowledge. You have either listened to gossip or, at the best, second or even third hand information."

"So, it's not true?"

"Certainly not. My advice to any young man – or, indeed, any young woman – who found themselves in Robert's situation would be to make a clean breast of the matter."

"In that case, can you explain why he left the office so hurriedly on that Monday morning? He arrived sometime after nine o'clock and was home again by midday."

"I do not see where your line of questioning is taking us, Mr Bingham."

"Somewhere between those two times, Robert learned of his dilemma. The only place that could have happened was here in the Treasury. Someone here would have known of what was alleged to have happened in advance and confronted him with the knowledge. At this point, I would have thought the police might have been informed and Robert apprehended for questioning, but this did not happen. Instead, he fled."

"I really do not feel I can be of much help to you, Mr Bingham …"

"Who would have confronted Robert on the fateful morning?"

"You are assuming he was *confronted*. He may well have discovered his *dilemma*, as you express it, through other means."

"Did you see him on that morning?"

Bingham knew that such men as he assumed Kevin Pierce to be would draw back from telling an actual lie: 'economical with the truth' – yes, but not an actual, barefaced lie. Perhaps it was part of their breeding, the years spent absorbing traditional values at public school, or perhaps it was a natural safeguard against possible future accusations in front of witnesses: Bingham was unsure, but he knew his adversary was deeply troubled.

"I do not recall passing more than a few words with him."

"Along what lines?"

"Really, Mr Bingham, I do feel we are getting nowhere with this rather insistent line of questioning."

"Nevertheless, you agreed to see me, presumably because you thought you might be of help in finding Robert?"

"Of course. Finding Robert is in all our interests. The sooner this matter is cleared up the better for everyone concerned."

"Knowing him as you do – as his immediate superior – do you believe him capable of theft?"

"Until he absconded, I would have placed my reputation on Robert being an honourable young man, but events, as they stand, would suggest otherwise. I can only wish you luck in your search, Mr Bingham. The sooner Robert is able to give an account of his behaviour, the better for all concerned."

It was a dismissal speech and the Executive Officer, acquainted as he was with his superior's methods, moved towards the door; but Bingham did not stir and Kevin Pierce rose only a mere inch. The two men sat watching each other as a deer, alerted to its fate, might for a moment or two watch the eyes of the hunter whose gun was pointing in its direction.

"You may take your break now, Colin. I'll see Mr Bingham to the door when the time comes."

The young man smiled but his eyes told Bingham he was upset at being shown the very door he'd expected to be opening for another. When it closed, Bingham said:

"Whoops!"

The Under Secretary continued the rise from his desk and turned to gaze from the window, which was to one side of where he sat, allowing daylight to fall naturally upon his work. The office looked out across Parliament Square: a pleasant enough view on most occasions, and one likely to distract a person's attention from the vicissitudes of the workplace. There was the large open green with trees to the west and statues of statesmen and other notables; it was also the venue for protests and demonstrations, which cannot have been to the civil servant's liking. Without turning to face Bingham, Kevin Pierce spoke.

"The report to which you refer is something I cannot discuss with you in any detail, Mr Bingham. Suffice to say that it involved a thorough investigation of certain concerns raised by Her Majesty's Revenue and Customs. These were discovered to be a mixture of unsubstantiated rumour, incorrect information or repetition of earlier allegations which had, at the time, been fully investigated and found to be unsupported by the facts."

"But Robert Courtney was very perturbed when he read the report – perturbed enough to bring it to your attention?"

"He did apprise me of its contents."

"And his knowledge of this report was instrumental in expediting his flight?"

"I do not follow your inference, Mr Bingham."

"With great respect, Mr Pierce, I think you do. I needed to confirm what I've been led to believe over the last few days, and you've been kind enough to do that for me. Thank you for your time."

It was Bingham who rose and stepped back towards the door, much to the Under-Secretary's surprise. Kevin Pierce turned and looked at his adversary, the expression in his eyes a mixture of consternation and fear, his Adam's apple on the move.

"I am pleased to have been of assistance, Mr Bingham."

Bingham inclined his head, more in acknowledgement of his departure than in any token of respect and closed the door behind him, leaving the Under Secretary with his back to the window.

Making his own way along the corridor towards the reception foyer, Bingham felt he'd cleared more scrub from the trail, while realising he was still as far from his quarry as he had been when Mabel Courtney first spoke with him.

Chapter Seven

THE MINISTER'S CLERK

It was late afternoon when Bingham emerged from
the Treasury. He was tired, worn-down and hungry:
feeling much like a stag must feel when the hunt has
been on its trail for most of the day.

He had, of course, merely unsettled Kevin Pierce, but
unsettling a person who had something to hide could be
guaranteed to create a disturbance somewhere. Would
the civil servant instigate a move now that the existence
of the report seemed to be more widely known, if only
to draw Robert Courtney back into what Dan Jessop
had referred to as 'the Whitehall Loop'? Bingham
thought so, and since he couldn't rely on Mariam Levy
and her associates to find Robert Courtney, he must
hope the authorities would be keener to flush him out.

One thing he was convinced of was Robert
Courtney's innocence; everything that had passed
between him and the Under Secretary suggested to
Bingham this was the case, and that those who had
spoken up for the young man were right to trust him.
Meeting Kevin Pierce had settled Bingham's mind, and
was also leading it along other paths.

There was as yet, no accounting for the money that
Robert appeared to have purloined, but Bingham saw
that as a side issue. The crux of the matter resided in the

report, and the nature of its embarrassment for the Under Secretary.

With the journalist, Lionel Bliss, hungry for a story, Bingham felt that serious moves could be made to establish what had happened.

There was nothing more to do that day, except return to Cecilia's flat and have a nap. Despite being retired, Bingham had the Friday feeling; picking up a copy of *Metro* to read on the Tube, he realised that it was, in fact, Friday, and that he'd been in London for five days and wanted to go home to his dogs.

The hunt for Robert Courtney seemed, irritatingly, to be in the hands of other people over that long weekend as they waited for news to arrive from Mariam Levy or for the Under Secretary to show his hand. Bingham had phoned Lionel Bliss and brought him up to date with events, hoping to whet his appetite and have him alert and ready for the chase. All he and Lina had left to do was hang fire. Throughout the two days, one of them was always in their daughter's flat waiting for the phone to ring. Finally, early on the Monday morning it did.

"Mr Bingham, we are ready for you now."

It was Mariam Levy's voice, and Bingham heaved a sigh of relief. He'd wanted to rouse Kevin Pierce and had needed to satisfy his mind on the issue of Robert's guilt, but Bingham much preferred that he, rather than the authorities, should find the fugitive.

He stepped outside into a London refreshed by the weekend rain but which was now warming up again. Russell Square to Holborn, Holborn to Mile End: Bingham felt he was becoming a local. The underground train was less humid that previously, but the day was young and there was time for the heat to build into an unpleasant congealing of human odour and unseasonable weather.

At Mile End he made his way to Mariam Levy's flat. It was only as he turned out of Bow Common Lane that he realised a man he'd barely noticed on the underground train was behind him. He was a young man, dressed in jeans and a leather jacket over a T-shirt. There was no reason why he shouldn't be following Bingham, of course: he might well live in the area. But Bingham felt he'd seen him somewhere before. To Bingham's mind, neither the style of dress nor the young man's presence rang true.

He paused on the corner and pretended to consult the map on his mobile phone, while the man walked on. Only the man didn't: he passed Bingham, and then turned to speak.

"You looking for somewhere, guv?"

Bingham gazed into the face that watched him, smiling. The eyes weren't the eyes of someone who used the word 'guv' in normal speech or who felt comfortable wearing a leather jacket over a T-shirt.

"I'm looking up a friend, and I thought she said she'd moved to ... Portia Crescent," he replied, hoping the hesitation wasn't too apparent. It was one of the places he thought Lina had mentioned.

"Ah ... just a minute ... let's look at your map ...," said the young man, easing the phone from Bingham's fingers. "Here we are ... a bit further on down the lane and to your right."

"Thank you."

"It's a pleasure. No problem."

With a wave and a cheery smile, the young man strode on, leaving Bingham standing on the corner. He cursed himself for jumping to conclusions about people he didn't know, but just in case he had been right in his assumptions, Bingham walked on and bided his time in Portia Crescent before turning back to Burley Close.

Vera was nowhere to be seen, and Bingham made his way through the back courtyard to the door of number 4B – with its green, peeling paint – unaided. This time, Mariam Levy opened it with a smile: a nervous smile but a smile, nonetheless. She glanced around and then ushered Bingham back down the stairs to the yard, looking about her all the while.

Bingham knew that Stan Chalfont would be watching but there was no sign of him. The girl led Bingham to the courtyard, dodging the washing on the lines, and it was then Bingham noticed the van with its distinctive lettering: Smart Image Dry Cleaning.

"My friends will take you to him now. Their English is not good, but they understand."

Bingham took this to mean that he was not to ask too many questions – if any – and walked over to the van. A young man stepped from the driver's seat, smiled, opened the rear doors and indicated that Bingham should climb inside. It was clean – as one might expect from a laundry van, thought Bingham – but promised a rough ride despite a few bags of washing one might lean on stacked against the sides. Still looking around her, still throwing Bingham quick, nervous smiles, Mariam made her way back to her flat as the van pulled out towards Burley Close.

Two things happened as he watched from the rear window: Stan Chalfont emerged and made his way rapidly down the back stairs, meeting Mariam on the way up, and the young man in the jeans and leather jacket appeared around the corner of the flats.

Bingham groaned. He had been followed. What a fool he'd been to have carried on to the girl's flat. He didn't doubt now that the man was some kind of policeman, probably from what Dan Jessop had called Special Branch in that rather long-winded explanation. It wouldn't take much for him to get Stan Chalfont talking. He felt immediately sorry for Mariam, who seemed to have done nothing but help a fugitive.

For a week nothing had happened and now everything was on the move. Had the Special Branch man anything to do with his visit to Kevin Pierce? Somehow, Bingham didn't doubt this to be so. He'd been watched that morning, if not over the entire weekend.

"Lina," he said, phoning her rapidly, "Get on to Lionel Bliss. Tell him to make his way to Burley Close …Yes, of course it's me."

"I can't hear you very clearly."

"What? I mean pardon."

"I can't hear you very clearly."

"Stop the van," yelled Bingham, tapping the driver on the shoulder through the mesh screen."

"What?"

"The van! Stop the van! Pull over!"

Anxious glances passed between the two men, the driver and his companion, but they did as Bingham urged. He opened the rear doors and clambered out.

"Can you hear me now, Lina?"

"Yes. What's happened?

"I'll explain later. Phone Lionel Bliss and ask him to get over to Burley Close. If he has a car, it would be very useful. Let's go!"

His last remark was fired at the two men. He pulled himself back into the van, the doors were slammed and off they went. Agitation had now, understandably, set in. Efficient as he was with European languages, Bingham knew no Arabic. The two men chattered among themselves, threw Bingham angry glances and drove on.

Bingham tried to picture the scene in Burley Close. The Special Branch man would have wrenched what he needed to know immediately from Chalfont and was no doubt questioning Mariam. Since it was certain that Stan wouldn't know where the van was heading and the girl probably didn't either, what could the policeman do? What would he do in such circumstances? Alert a patrol car and have them followed; it was the only option.

After what Bingham thought was a mile or two, the van pulled into another courtyard, like the one behind Mariam's block of flats. Without ceremony – indeed, roughly – the two men hastened Bingham from the van and, keeping his head down, steered him along an alleyway, through a narrow door and up a flight of interior steps.

A door was opened hurriedly, and he found himself in a shabby flat. One glance told his orderly mind 'men without women'. Dirty plates and used food packages were everywhere, cluttered between cans of fizzy drinks. Sunlight and late-in-the-season flies made their way in through an open window. In a side room, Bingham noticed an unmade bed; a pillow had been flung on the floor beside a cup of unfinished coffee. There was no sign of anything homely such as an ornament or a bowl of fruit. Even the chairs, which looked as if they'd been retrieved from a waste tip, so ill-matched were they, lacked comfort. Here, men slept and ate but didn't live in any domestic sense.

The driver nodded Bingham to one of the chairs, a cane one without a cushion, while his companion locked the door. Fear emerged from them like sweat as they made several phone calls. Bingham caught only one name – Mariam. At least, then, they were in touch with what was happening in Burley Close.

The driver's companion opened a can of cola and nodded Bingham an offer of one; he refused as politely as he could, as the man opened another for his friend. The phone calls continued but Bingham made out only one more name, Farid, which was repeated several times, as was Mariam's. He guessed from this that the driver had phoned only two people and, therefore, two places.

Anxiety was in the tone of each call and as they progressed the driver looked at Bingham with increasing consternation. These men, like Mariam, had fled persecution in their own countries; their lives had encouraged them to trust no one. The driver gestured Bingham to the phone.

"You must return immediately," said a voice.

"Who is this?" asked Bingham.

"It's me, Mariam. You must return immediately."

"What do you mean?"

"I've told him …," said Mariam, her voice faint as though she had turned away from the phone.

"Pardon?" said Bingham.

"I'm talking to someone else, Mr Bingham ... Yes. All right, I understand ... Mr Bingham, you must come back."

"I don't understand. What's happened?"

"Hang up? Yes, of course. I must go, Mr Bingham. Come quickly."

Bingham handed the phone back to the driver, making a gesture to ask whether the man understood. He nodded and made for the door.

The return journey was undertaken in silence; sadness rather than agitation was its keynote. The two Syrians barely spoke, and then only in whispers. Bingham was left wondering why he'd been driven to an empty flat.

As the van pulled into the courtyard of the Burley Close, Bingham's sense of disaster tightened in his throat. The area around the flats was crowded with people, obviously urged on by curiosity. A police car was drawn up against the pavement opposite the Smart Image Dry Cleaners. Vera came up to the van, her face tearstained.

"You'd better come this way," she said, "They're waiting for you."

Lionel Bliss was hovering outside the launderette. He called across to Bingham, as though he'd been waiting for him. Together they made their way through the crowd which was pushing against a police barrier but not daring to cross the blue and white tape. A policeman, his face controlled, was apparently standing guard at the bottom of the flight of stairs that led to the flat above the launderette.

"Mr Bingham?" he asked.

"Yes."

"Come this way, sir."

Bingham was led into a tent-like structure. Somehow, he already knew what he was going to see but that didn't lessen the shock.

A young man lay sprawled on the ground. His arms and legs were twisted outwards from his body, one arm and leg facing upwards and the others stretched down, hands and one foot uplifted. One side of his skull was shattered, the bones of his face broken; the jaw was tilted at a peculiar angle, as though the boy had died complaining.

Bingham could not think of him as other than a boy; he was the same age as his youngest son.

"Can you identify him, sir?"

"Yes," Bingham lied, for he hadn't seen Robert Courtney in years.

But he knew. There could be no doubt that the body he was looking at was the young man he was seeking.

"Do you mind if I make a phone call?"

"Who to, sir?" asked another officer, obviously senior in rank to the guard.

"My wife."

"Of course, sir," replied the policeman, standing close while Bingham made the call.

"Lina, I want you to get the first train possible home ... Yes, it is bad news, and I want you to be there ... Yes ... It'll be in the morning papers, and if you can get to Mabel first, it will be a comfort. I'll give you the details later ... Yes, I don't think she needs to know too much at this stage."

Bingham turned to the senior policeman who nodded his understanding.

"I'll see to it, sir, but we shall need to know that the next of kin has been informed."

"May I go?"

As Bingham left, the forensic team arrived. He made his way across to Mariam Levy, who was still standing with the crowd of her neighbours on the stretch of pavement outside their flats.

"May I have a word?"

She followed him up to her flat. Bingham was surprised at her composure. He'd expected tears but was offered, quite calmly, a cup of tea. Watching her set the cups, the sugar bowl and milk jug in front of him, Bingham tried to imagine what horrors could have inured a young woman to violent death; but he read the papers, and, somehow, he knew.

"What happened after I left?"

"Mr Chalfont came out and started talking to the man in the leather jacket and jeans. He'd seen them bring Robert to the launderette on Sunday night ..."

"Then why was I driven somewhere else?"

"We didn't want to take any chances with being tricked. We thought if you were led away, you could be brought back when we were sure no one else was coming. Do you understand?"

"Yes. Go on."

"The man in the leather jacket went up to the flat over the launderette. Farid, who runs the cleaners, tried to stop him, but it was no use. He banged on the door over and over again, but Robert would not come out and so he attacked the door, trying to smash it open. Then the police car arrived. The sirens were blaring, and they rushed across to the launderette. I didn't see anything else."

"So, the man in the leather jacket broke into the flat before the police arrived?"

"Oh yes, I think so."

"And the police followed him in/"

"Yes."

"How soon after?"

"Very soon. The door of the flat was smashed open, and then they ran up the stairs."

"I'm sorry you and your friends have become involved. It was very kind of you."

"Will there be trouble?"

"I hope not. It depends on … "

What did it depend on? Bingham wasn't sure, and there was no point in making empty promises. He wondered whether he'd be allowed into the flat Robert Courtney had occupied for just one night; there might be items he would need. He said as much to Mariam.

She went into the kitchenette, returning with a brown paper envelope.

"Robert left this with me. He said it would be safe here if ever he was caught."

"Why didn't you give it to me before?"

"Robert was alive then, and I had no reason to trust you."

It was true. No one had any reason to suppose Robert had ever stayed in Mariam's flat – no one except Stan Chalfont. How much had he told the man in the jeans and leather jacket? Bingham knew what the envelope contained. He tucked it under his jacket and walked down into the street.

Lionel Bliss was waiting for him, expectation in every line of his face and angle of his body. He knew he'd been summoned as an agent of the free press: a deterrent against official secrecy. He said so.

"Have you got your story?"

"I've a few columns worth. Have you anything else to tell me?"

"Possibly. Give me a call later today. I've things to think about."

"Who called the police?"

"The man in the jeans and leather jacket might be able to answer that question. As far as I know, he's still in the flat. Go and ask him."

Bingham waited, his mind a whirl: so much to think about, to anticipate, so many unanswered questions, so many people to out-think. When Lionel Bliss returned his face was downcast.

"They're turning the flat over. They told me to piss off."

The two men looked at each other, sharing a single thought: there was nothing more to be gained by hanging round in Burley Close.

"Can I give you a lift?"

"Thanks," replied Bingham, "That would be appreciated."

Bingham took no notice of the drive back to his daughter's home; the complications of driving through central London passed him by. When Lionel Bliss pulled up by the Bloomsbury flat, Bingham said:

"It's not my business to tell you what to write, Lionel, but I do think you should go easy on Mariam and her friends. They're not criminals. They were only trying to help."

"They were helping a criminal. Wasn't there something in it for them?"

"They're refugees. They've presumably survived what Dylan called 'the unarmed route of flight', and they're working for a living. Give them a break."

"I write what earns me a living, George, and that's what sells newspapers."

"At least give me a few hours before you submit any copy. I may have something more interesting."

"Like?"

"Give me a few hours. I'll ring you when I know."

The journalist looked at Bingham as though he doubted his every word. Bingham clambered out of the car. He watched Lionel Bliss drive off and turned to Cecilia's flat.

It was only then he embraced the awful fact that Robert Courtney was dead; it was at that moment the shock came home to rest. Standing on the pavement, he was reminded of the day his father died; everyone had been so busy with the details that it was only when he had left his mother and was driving home that Bingham grasped the truth of what had happened, of what all the arrangements had been about, only then that the tears came.

He couldn't go in and face Bruno, not feeling as he did, but where could he find a quiet spot? Russell Square Gardens – that was the place. He'd find a seat and sit out his sorrow, just for a while, not too long; there was work to do, decisions to be made, but he had to give himself just that little bit of time alone.

Bingham found a seat and removed his hearing aids, effectively cutting himself off from the clusters of people around; encroaching deafness had its advantages at times. He sat for a moment allowing the sorrow of the young man's death to soak through him, but there it stayed. How responsible had he been for the death, and how responsible was he now for involving those who had helped Robert Courtney? The young man had died with dishonour attached to his name, and Mabel Courtney had lost an only, beloved son. Had anything been achieved by his pursuit?

Bingham removed the brown envelope from inside his coat where he'd tucked it and began to skip read the contents of the report it contained, presumably the report that had sent Robert Courtney on the road of flight.

Bingham's many isolated perceptions came together. He could not bring back the dead, but there might just be something he could achieve to alleviate the wrongs that had been set in motion. His mind clear, Bingham made his way to the Treasury, calling off first at Liverpool Street Station where he purchased writing paper and envelopes from W H Smith, wrote a brief note to Sir Herbert Elliot and paid a call to the Excess Baggage Company on platform 10.

Chapter Eight
THE PERMANENT UNDER SECRETARY

Bingham found a seat in St James's Park and waited. The doorman in his reflective body-warmer had been only too pleased to call out one of the receptionists who graced Bingham with a frown but promised to have his letter delivered to Sir Herbert "assuming Sir Herbert is in the building". Bingham stressed that even if he were not, it would be in the Permanent Under Secretary's interests to receive his note "immediately if not sooner". It wasn't a phrase known to her generation and the frown deepened, but something in Bingham's manner must have indicated urgency because it was no more than fifteen minutes after he'd found a seat conveniently placed to watch the Treasury that a young man, slim and graceful with a mass of black hair and smartly dressed in a pin-stripe suit, approached him.

"Mr Bingham?"

It was a question, but the young man's tone suggested he was certain of the answer. Bingham smiled, both to himself and the young man, thinking that these people wouldn't understand what it was to lack confidence; in fact, they oozed it. Breeding and then appropriate schooling saw to their suitability to rule the country and, at one time, the world. He thought of Robert Courtney: in the Loop but not of it.

Sir Herbert Elliot's office was almost identical to that of the Under Secretary, Kevin Pierce: larger as, perhaps, befitted his permanent status but resplendent in the beauty of its panelling and furniture. Bingham's knowledge of antiques was sketchy but he appreciated the skills involved in the art of the cabinet maker.

"Mr Bingham, I am pleased to make your acquaintance. Your fame precedes you."

The extended hand was firm and warm, the hand of a man you could trust. Bingham smiled; his fame rested on two cases – his part in the third having been kept discreet – and he wasn't aware that his first had attracted too much attention nationally. These people didn't seem to miss a trick. How on earth did this Permanent Under Secretary to the Treasury come to know?

"Please sit down. I am sorry to have kept you waiting. I understand you have news concerning this unfortunate young man, Mr Robert Courtney."

"What I have to say will be of a confidential nature. Are you happy for me to speak in the presence of your Executive Officer?"

"Eh, Higher Executive Officer," replied Sir Herbert with a smile and a twinkle of his grey eyes, "Oh yes, Nigel is the soul of discretion."

The very senior civil servant graced his colleague with a broad smile. Bingham wondered whether the slim young man with the mass of dark hair would one day earn himself a place where Sir Herbert now sat, stout and with a neatly coiffured head of iron-grey hair. Bingham looked at the Permanent Under Secretary and noted the large head and reddish complexion – the face of a drinker, his mother would have said, but a drinker of the finest Scotch, thought Bingham.

"In that case, I'd like to sketch out for you the series of events that led to Robert's death," said Bingham.

"Please go ahead."

"Robert Courtney was involved on a project that gave him access to certain very confidential information. I have the impression that his work was in some way connected with the civil service's unenviable task, brought about by the results of this year's wretched referendum that has obliged us to find ways of ending our commitment to Europe.

He was used to having access to such documents and, clearly, he was trusted to respect their confidentiality. Anyone but a complete fool would see the need for certain information to remain secret. A lot of damage is done by the irresponsible handling of delicate information by the press; and if you're dealing with a public many of whom only read the headlines then diplomacy is of the essence."

Bingham saw the smiles pass between the Permanent Under Secretary and his Higher Executive Officer. Here was a man, they thought, who saw the need for judiciousness; and that was the impression Bingham wished to convey.

"However, we're talking here of diplomacy in the national interest, and not diplomacy in the interests of the civil service, politicians or any other public servant; especially if such diplomacy hides incompetence and corruption, which the report in question – the one jocularly called *Whoop/s* – did."

The smiles faded, the Higher Executive Officer fidgeted and the Permanent Under Secretary coughed; indeed, Sir Herbert, against his better judgement, was obliged to ask:

"Have you read the report in question, Mr Bingham?"

"Let us suppose for the sake of argument that I have," Bingham replied, cautiously, "but it doesn't matter as far as the sequence of events I am outlining is concerned. The point is that Robert Courtney came across this report and was shocked by its contents. He saw no reason why it should not be made public; indeed, he believed it was morally right to do so.

He could, of course, have gone straight to the press – become a whistle-blower – but he didn't. He did the honourable thing – he went to his superior officer and made his concerns and recommendations clear. Whether or not Kevin Pierce passed these concerns on I do not know. What I suspect is that he advised Robert Courtney to think carefully about what he was recommending. The young man, however, had no doubt what the right course of action should be, and said so.

A weekend intervened and when Robert Courtney returned to work on the Monday morning, still determined to expose the contents of the report, he was told to lay low for a while, no doubt until matters could be "handled appropriately". I can almost hear the phrase being spoken. He trusted his senior officer and took garden leave, as the phrase goes.

What he didn't know was that over the weekend a bank account opened in his name had been credited with a quarter-of-a-million pounds and that a press release had been prepared suggesting he had absconded with the money. In short, he was deliberately discredited, an action that would cast doubt on any assertions he might later make.

His mother's home was ransacked – not because anything was expected to be concealed there because

Robert hadn't returned home that weekend, but simply to give the impression that the authorities had a genuine concern about the young man's activities and political views. Similarly, his flat in Holborn was searched – this time more carefully because he might have had the chance to hide something.

When he left the flat, he was unsure where to go, but as luck – or ill-luck – would have it, he was shown sympathy by a Syrian refugee, a young woman from whom he always bought his weekly copy of *The Big Issue*.

For a while I was confused about the role of the refugees in this matter. I wasn't sure whether they saw themselves as having their hands on a situation that could be exploited, and I wasn't sure whether the authorities knew about their helping Robert. Today's events clarified both doubts – but I'll come to that later.

Robert was now on the run – essentially a criminal – and this was just what was required by those eager to keep the contents of the report secret. In a sense, there was almost no need to catch him: his remaining a permanent fugitive would suffice. Eventually, he might make his way abroad, and this would only discredit him further.

Imagine him, now, living among strangers, some of whom barely spoke his language – a young man used to order surviving in a chaotic world, a young man betrayed (or, at the best, ignored) by those he'd considered friends. He became more and more isolated, cut off from the world he knew, unable to contact anyone who might have helped him.

And now we come to the events of last week. Two things occurred that moved matters on: I put the wind-up Kevin Pierce by giving the impression I knew more than I did at that time – although what I suspected was to be confirmed later – and I suggested to the *Big Issue* vendor that if she really wanted to help Robert Courtney, it would be in his interests for us to find him rather than the authorities.

By this time, I'd concluded that nothing could be resolved until he was found, and I'd obtained sufficient information to help clear his name."

Bingham made a silent apology to Lina for this half-truth before continuing.

"This morning, I received a phone call from the young woman telling me that Robert had been found and agreed to see me. I was then followed to my destination by a police officer from Special Branch who could only have been put in position by Kevin Pierce or someone who had listened to an account of my interview with him. As I was driven away on what I later learned had been a precautionary diversion, the Special Branch officer broke into the flat where Robert was hiding.

When I was returned to Burley Close it became clear that Robert had tried to evade arrest and subsequently fallen from the balcony, had committed suicide or been pushed to his death. Over to you, Sir Herbert."

During Bingham's long and detailed account, the Permanent Under Secretary had displayed no emotion, except when Bingham mentioned the report by name, and his features, sagging with age, had hidden quite effectively what he might have been thinking. Bingham knew what was going through his mind: the reputation of the Treasury must be protected at all costs and I will only offer a soothing hand here if my department's interests are not adversely affected by my doing so.

The face of Sir Herbert's Higher Executive Officer exhibited the same concern.

"I really must congratulate you on your very succinct account, Mr Bingham. Had you not already earned a well-deserved retirement from your work in the Education Service, I would be tempted to offer you a post in the public relations department of the Treasury."

Bingham smiled but said nothing. Lina had always said he was immune to flattery and it was certainly true at that moment.

"Perhaps we could examine your account analytically? But first, let me offer you tea. It seems that time of the day has come around again. Nigel, would you be kind enough to do the honours?"

Sir Herbert favoured Bingham with another smile as his Higher Executive Officer picked up the internal phone.

"The great shame is that this whole, unfortunate episode wasn't nipped in the bud earlier, Mr Bingham. Such a tragedy – a young life lost unnecessarily and in extremely unpleasant circumstances. One's heart goes out to his friends and family."

"I think that failure rests with your department, Sir Herbert."

"Yes, I can see why you would say that, although – having listened to your ... *account* – I am not sure that an outsider would see it in the same light. I admire you, Mr Bingham. You are an honourable man, and one who possesses an admirable tenacity, but I'm afraid your view of events is somewhat clouded by your quite natural prejudices."

Bingham said nothing to help a man who, it seemed to him, was concocting an alternative view of the events leading to Robert Courtney's death before his very eyes.

"You knew Robert Courtney as a boy, didn't you? He grew up in the village where you live and, presumably, went to the same school as your own children. I would imagine that he may even have been in the same class as one of them, so close was his age to theirs."

"He was in the same year group as my youngest son, Ben."

"Quite – and so you started your investigation quite convinced of his innocence. Why wouldn't you? You'd seen him grow up. You know his mother. Once you started from that assumption, everything else fell into place. It would have been difficult, I believe, to persuade you that he was guilty."

"You're quite wrong in supposing any such thing, and even if you were right it wouldn't account for the fact that everyone who knew Robert, including Kevin Pierce, has spoken well of him."

A discreet tap on the door was followed by a smart, elderly lady pushing a small, hostess trolley replete with a bone china tea set, the pot steaming gently, and a selection of fondant creams.

"Ah, Mrs Hainsworth – Gladys – always a welcome sight at four o'clock on any afternoon. Nigel will see to the honours. Thank you."

The lady favoured Bingham with a smile, nodded discreetly and left. The pouring of the tea and associated questions concerning milk and sugar took their time – not deliberately to allow Sir Herbert to collect his arguments, thought Bingham, but in accordance with the normal ritual.

"It would hardly be otherwise, would it, Mr Bingham? One's friends and family will always speak up for one – and Kevin Pierce has always possessed what one might term a dogged protectiveness towards his young men. Admirable *but* … not always well rewarded."

"If I might say so, Sir Herbert, your view of this chain of events is as selective as you accuse mine of being. Many of Robert's friends, as you call them, barely knew him, but every one of them spoke up for him …"

"Mr Bingham excuse my interruption but I must correct the expression 'your view'. I can assure you that any committee of enquiry set up to review this unfortunate case would come to a similar conclusion. The facts speak for themselves and it is the facts upon which any judgement would be made."

Above all things, thought Bingham, the Treasury would want to avoid a committee of enquiry; it's interesting that I have asked for nothing of the kind, and yet it is clearly foremost in this man's mind.

"Robert Courtney, whatever you might imply to the contrary, was a young man of excellent character. It is my view that the committee of enquiry to which you refer would take that into account when drawing their conclusions."

"I couldn't agree more, but they would also consider how well society has favoured Mr Courtney: grammar school, Oxford, Her Majesty's Civil Service! It's not every boy from a Suffolk village who rises to such heights. In my view, he would be seen to have spurned all that had been bestowed upon him."

Bingham knew there was no point in losing his temper or arguing against such convenient convictions. From what Dan Jessop had told him and from what

Lionel Bliss had indicated in his story of the soldier, Bingham knew that any such enquiry would be led by the likes of Sir Herbert Elliot, who would do everything in his power to persuade those who comprised the committee to see things his way.

"I think something else you must consider, Mr Bingham, is the nature of the company into which Mr Courtney fell after he'd run away. It may well be seen that he courted such company, that such company was in some way responsible for his theft of government funds. There is sufficient distrust of refugees in this country at this time to bring down opprobrium on the head of anyone who might be seen to be in league with them and their supposed intentions. You have said as much yourself."

"I said no such thing."

"Let me correct you, Mr Bingham. In your opening account you stated that you were *confused about the role of the refugees in this matter*, that you were not sure whether they saw themselves *as having their hands on a situation that could be exploited* if my memory serves me correctly."

"I meant that I couldn't rule out their involvement, not that …"

"Exactly! I was not suggesting prejudice on your part. In your case, it was merely a need to take all factors into account – as would be the case with any committee we might consider it necessary to set up – but it wouldn't be seen that way by the bigots, Mr Bingham. Robert Courtney would be tarred with the same brush. Not all our fellow citizens are liberal-minded."

Bingham sat subdued, cursing himself for a turn of phrase he'd not intended, and realising what his adversary would do with those people who had only helped Robert Courtney out of kindness.

"You are following my line of thinking, aren't you? Perhaps there was more to Mr Courtney than meets the eye? Like you, he was liberal-minded and such a young man would be appalled at the treatment we, as a nation, are dishing out to refugees at this time. Is it possible, then, that Mr Courtney decided to act? I am not suggesting that this is so, but that the mere suggestion would be enough to damn him in the eyes of the public. You can imagine the meal the right-wing press would make of his case, can you not? Even if a committee of enquiry cleared his name without a shadow of doubt, doubt would still linger in the public mind. Nothing sticks like mud, Mr Bingham."

"Except ...," replied Bingham, angry with himself, his adversary, and just about everyone else but disinclined to utter the word he had in mind.

"I, too, declined to use the image, but you are no doubt correct."

Bingham watched, feeling helpless, while the Higher Executive Officer poured him a second cup of tea and offered him another fondant cream. Sir Herbert's eyes never left Bingham's face. Uncomfortable and feeling beaten, Bingham rose and walked to the window. Kevin Pierce's office had overlooked Parliament Square – an interesting enough prospect; Sir Herbert's overlooked St James's Park, which was even more so.

Bingham gazed across the park at Duck Island, the Blue Bridge and beyond to Buckingham Palace and the Mall, where he had stood just a week ago admiring the statue of George the Sixth, a decent man. He wondered for the second time what the king who had taken his country through the Second World War would make of modern Britain.

"Don't be despondent, Mr Bingham. I am sure we will find a way through this maze. You are a romantic, are you not ... a righter of wrongs ... a musketeer, your blade bright and flashing? So are we all, in our own way, but the world only appreciates romantics on the screen; in real life, do they, often, not create more troubles than they solve?

Let us consider again the character of Robert Courtney. You knew him as a boy, but he has become a man. Have your children grown into the adults you and your wife would have wished?"

Bingham turned from the window and looked the senior civil servant in the face. He was proud of his children but it was true that he and Lina might have wished their daughters had been a little less wild, that their grandson had been born into a traditional family setup with a father present, that their younger son could find a girl he loved and settle down happily.

"All of us, as parents, believe in original innocence, do we not? But the other side of the coin is, of course, original sin – not a popular notion these days, but one to be considered. The point I am making is that many crimes are inexplicable because of the very fact that *we think we know the person who committed them*. But do we? How many times have you heard people – usually family and friends – say that they couldn't believe someone they thought they knew had behaved in a reprehensible manner?

I am suggesting that the little boy who grew up with loving parents in a tranquil village and was taught to believe all the right things by his teachers may have had demons working within him that moved his life in other directions. Is it not possible that he was corrupted as he grew older? Do circumstances not change people?"

It was true, of course, even in relatively small domestic ways. He and Lina saw little of their older son, Paul, now that he was married and with a family. The boy who had once been so close to them and was reputed, wrongly, to be Lina's favourite child spent more time with his wife's family than with them during holidays.

"We can never know what really motivates a person once they reach adulthood. We can just as easily prove the Robert Courtneys of this world guilty as we can prove them innocent. It's simply a question of whose view you accept – the prosecutions or that of the defence; and Robert Courtney will have as many detractors as he will have supporters. Do we want that to happen? This is the real world, Mr Bingham, and not the schoolroom."

With all the skill of a barrister intent of winning his case, Sir Herbert Elliot had not only taken Bingham's account apart, but he had also thrown into question Bingham's judgement and Robert Courtney's character, neither of which were really in dispute. But this was, as the Permanent Under Secretary had said, the real world. Bingham hated that phrase, and not only for its falseness.

"May I just take you in another direction? Mr Courtney at twenty-six is neither married nor has been known to have many female friends ..."

"That's enough! This is becoming ridiculous."

"I am merely trying to illustrate what the public view will be should this incident ever reach the papers ..."

"Yes, yes, I can see your drift. You are no doubt right. They would dig around for any story, however untrue, that might give them column inches."

"Precisely! What we are saying is that this incident must never enter the public domain ... *except as the unfortunate death of an estimable young man.*"

Bingham did not care to return to his chair but considered it sullen of him not to do so. He picked up his second cup of tea, which by now had gone cold.

"I think we understand each other, Mr Bingham. May I suggest that your purpose in coming here was threefold? Firstly, you wished to clear Mr Courtney's refugee friends of having anything criminal to do with his disappearance and death. Secondly, you wished to clear his name of any wrongdoing. Thirdly, you were concerned with the financial circumstances of Mrs Courtney, who – I believe – Robert helped from his salary. Would I be correct in my suppositions?"

"Near enough."

"In which case, I think we can come to an arrangement. A word in the right ears will prevent any scurrilous press articles concerning our refugee friends: in this case, it might be argued that there are issues of security."

"You mean a D Notice."

"More or less. They are vulnerable people in the present climate. Whereas generalisations cannot be prevented, the naming of individuals is to be deplored in case they provoke racist outbreaks.

Secondly, a suitably worded item in a reputable newspaper will exonerate Mr Courtney completely of any wrongdoing. We shall raise questions as where such leaks originated and set-in motion a line of enquiry to discover the culprits.

Thirdly, since Mr Courtney died in service it would be only appropriate to fund a small pension for his mother who was grateful for her son's generosity while he lived.

I think these measures address your concerns, do they not?"

"Yes, in the immediate sense."

"Do you know, Mr Bingham, I misjudged you. From the tone of your note, I rather received the impression that you might be tempted to exert a little pressure. It was only when I met you that I realised an honourable romantic like yourself would never consider stooping to such a tactic – a tactic that could only be counter-productive and undo all we have achieved."

"You may sleep undisturbed tonight, Sir Herbert."

"I am pleased to hear it, Mr Bingham. Now, if you've finished your tea, perhaps I could walk you to the door."

This offer raised the eyebrows of the Higher Executive Officer, and Bingham realised he was being afforded a great honour that broke the traditions of the establishment. Sir Herbert even strolled across Horse Guards Road and stood for a while in conversation with his visitor.

"I would wish you to believe what I said at the outset of our conversation, Mr Bingham – that it was a great shame this whole, unfortunate episode wasn't nipped in the bud earlier. I would like you to understand that I knew nothing of what was happening until *after* Mr Courtney had taken flight."

The two men shook hands, and Bingham watched the Permanent Under Secretary return to his place of work. Against his inclinations, Bingham believed what the man had said, but wondered whether the outcome would have been the same if Robert Courtney had been more than the son of a railway worker and a bank clerk.

Chapter Nine

THE MOTHER

The funeral in the little churchyard of St Mary Magdalene in Northfield attracted a large congregation, and among the many villagers and school-friends were a refugee who worked as a *Big Issue* vendor and a Permanent Under Secretary to the Treasury.

As promised, a carefully worded leak had been made by a well-regarded press officer. It was a copy of a letter from a Mr Kevin Pierce to a security officer in the Treasury deploring 'previous misrepresentation that suggested Mr Robert Courtney was other than a highly respected, eminently efficient, admirably conscientious young man engaged upon an important and vital project for Her Majesty's Treasury. To suggest otherwise was to impugn the reputation of someone who might have been seen as a future Under Secretary'. Mr Pierce went on to urge 'a thorough investigation of the misinformation previously leaked that led to the vilification by the press of a devoted civil servant'.

The article by Lionel Bliss surrounding the leak made no mention of the scene of Robert Courtney's death or of his associates at the time; it dwelt instead upon the 'terrible and unfortunate accident that nipped so promising a young life in the bud'. It contained an account of interviews with several witnesses who all expressed sorrow at the news and a liking for the young man who had 'always seemed so friendly'. Bingham didn't doubt Stan and Vera were among their number.

It was enough for Mabel Courtney, who felt her son had been "vindicated and his name cleared" when she sat with Bingham and Lina in her little kitchen overlooking the cottage garden in Lower Road. Coffee was brewing on the stove and fresh scones were awaiting butter on the little table with its gingham cloth.

After reading the article, Mabel Courtney showed Bingham the letter she'd received from Sir Herbert.

Dear Mrs Courtney,

It was with great sorrow that I received the news of your son's unfortunate accident. He was an admirable young man, greatly respected at the Treasury for his acumen and diligence.

At the time of his accident, Robert was engaged upon an important project for the Treasury involving our future economic relationship with the European Union. He had taken garden leave so that he might be free from the distractions of everyday office life to concentrate upon this vital work more fully.

I realise that my condolences will be of little comfort to you at this time, when your sorrow at the loss of your son will be uppermost in your mind, but I do hope that in time to come the news that Robert was so greatly appreciated by his colleagues will be of some small comfort.

With every good wish,
Yours sincerely,

Herbert Elliot

"It's a very kind letter, is n't it, George?" she'd said.

"Yes, it is," replied Bingham, struck by the lack of Sir Herbert's title under his signature, perhaps indicating that the letter had been written by a human being rather than a mere civil servant.

"They've given me a small pension as well. They said Robert had earned it by his hard work. It was very generous of Sir Herbert."

The service was a traditional one, following the pattern of all others before it: a simple committal to the Lord's care and a time for grieving. "I am the resurrection and the life … and whosoever believeth in me shall never die." The Reverend Clemency Freeman's powerful voice resounded throughout the church, while the angels in the nave and the kings and queens in the chancel looked down. The hymn they'd sung at Robert's christening, *Lord of All Hopefulness*, came first and *The Day Thou Gave Us Lord Is Ended* completed the ceremony.

At the graveside – where each day for her remaining years Mabel would come, sit, pray and refresh Robert's flowers, thinking of the boy she'd lost and the man he might have become – the young man's body was committed "… earth to earth, ashes to ashes, dust to dust; in sure and certain hope of the Resurrection to eternal life …".

Bingham and Lina looked at each other, she with her faith and he with his doubts, both wondering whether this was all we could truly expect: that one day justice would be done, if not here on Earth then in some other, better place.

In the meantime, the report that had outraged Robert Courtney was locked in a drawer at Bob's Farm, biding its time in the interests of the day.

Autumn 2016

ACKNOWLEDGEMENTS

Although this story is a fiction, its key events and descriptions are based on actual incidents and the experiences of people involved in similar situations and circumstances. Anyone wishing to delve deeper into the real world from which this novel is drawn should read:

Ministries of Deception: Cover-ups in Whitehall by Tim Slessor

Aurum Press Ltd 2002

All the characters in the book are fictitious, and any resemblance to persons living or dead, is purely coincidental.